harold

and

maude

a novel

colin higgins

CHICAGO
REVIEW
PRESS

This edition published in 2015 by
Chicago Review Press Incorporated
814 North Franklin Street
Chicago, Illinois 60610
ISBN 978-1-61373-126-0

Library of Congress Cataloging-in-Publication Data
Higgins, Colin, 1941–1988.
  Harold and Maude : a novel / Colin Higgins.
    pages ; cm
  ISBN 978-1-61373-126-0 (softcover)
  I. Title.

  PS3558.I355H28 2015
  813'.54—dc23
                                      2015002302

Cover design: Natalya Balnova
Interior design: Jonathan Hahn

Printed in the United States of America
5 4 3 2 1

"It's *very* provoking," Humpty Dumpty said after a long silence, looking away from Alice as he spoke, "to be called an egg,—*very!*"

Through the Looking-Glass
LEWIS CARROLL

HAROLD CHASEN STEPPED UP on the chair and placed the noose about his neck. He pulled it tight and tugged on the knot. It would hold. He looked about the den. The Chopin was playing softly. The envelope was propped up on the desk. Everything was ready. He waited. Outside, a car pulled into the driveway. It stopped, and he heard his mother get out. With barely a smile he knocked over the chair and fell jerkily into space. In a few moments his feet had stopped kicking, and his body swayed with the rope.

Mrs. Chasen put her keys down on the entrance table and called to the maid to take the packages out of the car. It had been a boring luncheon and she was tired. She looked at herself in the mirror and absently pushed at her hair. The frosted wig would be fine for dinner this evening, she decided. She'd cancel her appointment with René and take a nap for the rest of the afternoon. After all, she deserved to indulge herself once in a while. She went into the den and sat at the desk. As she flipped through her book for the hairdresser's number, she listened to the Chopin playing softly. How soothing, she thought, and began to dial. René would be furious but it couldn't be helped. The phone buzzed, and she settled back, drumming her fingers on the arm of the chair. She noticed on the desk the envelope addressed to her. She looked up and saw, suspended from the ceiling, the hanging body of her son.

She paused.

The body swayed slightly from side to side, making the rope around the large oak beam squeak rhythmically to the sound of the piano.

Mrs. Chasen stared at the bulging eyes, at the protruding tongue, at the knot stretched tight about the grotesquely twisted neck.

"I'm sorry," said a tiny voice. "You have reached a disconnected number. Please be sure you are dialing the right number and are dialing correctly. This is . . ."

Mrs. Chasen put down the phone. "Really, Harold," she said as she dialed again. "I suppose you think this is all very funny. Apparently it means nothing to you that the Crawfords are coming to dinner."

"OH, HAROLD WAS *ALWAYS* a well-mannered boy," said Mrs. Chasen to the elderly Mrs. Crawford at dinner that evening. "Yes, indeed. I had him using a little knife and fork at three. He was never any trouble as a baby, although he was perhaps more susceptible to illness than the average child. He probably got that from his father, because I've never been sick a day in my life. And, of course, he did inherit his father's strange sense of values—that *penchant* for the absurd. I remember once we were in Paris, Charlie stepped out for some cigarettes and the next thing I heard, he was arrested for floating nude down the Seine—experimenting in river currents with a pair of yellow rubber water wings. Well, that cost quite a bit of *enfluence* and *d'argent* to hush up, I can tell you."

The younger Mrs. Crawford laughed appreciatively, as did Mr. Crawford, Mr. Fisher, and Mr. and Mrs. Truscott-Jones. The elderly Mrs. Crawford sipped her champagne and smiled.

"Are you ready for dessert?" Mrs. Chasen asked her. "Is everyone ready for a delightful Peach Melba? Harold, dear, you haven't finished your beets."

Harold looked up from the end of the table.

"Did you hear me, dear? Eat up your beets. They're very nutritious. Very good for the system."

Harold looked at his mother and then quietly put down his fork.

"What ever is the matter?" asked Mrs. Chasen. "Aren't you feeling well?"

"I have a sore throat," he said softly.

"Oh, dear. Then perhaps you'd best go up to bed immediately. Excuse yourself and say good night to everyone."

"Excuse me," said Harold, "and good night everyone." He got up from the table and left the room.

"Good night," everyone echoed.

"Take some aspirin," Mrs. Chasen called after him. "And lots of water." She turned back to her guests. "Dear me," she said, "I don't know what I'm going to do with that boy. Lately he's become quite trying. I'm sending him to Dr. Harley, my psychiatrist, and, of course, my brother Victor—the brigadier general—keeps telling me the Army is the answer. But I don't want him off in some jungle battling natives. That's how I lost Charlie. Of course, Charlie wasn't battling. He was photographing parrots in Polynesia when that—"

"More champagne!" cried the elderly Mrs. Crawford, and burped.

"Mother!" said young Mrs. Crawford.

"Mother, please!" said Mr. Crawford.

"I'm sorry," said the elderly Mrs. Crawford. "I thought I saw a bat."

A momentary silence overtook the table until Mr. Truscott-Jones said that he had never tasted such a wonderful Peach Melba, and Mrs. Chasen told the story of how she had got the original recipe from a tenor in Tokyo who claimed to be Dame Nellie's bastard son.

WHY THEY BRING THAT OLD WOMAN to parties, thought Mrs. Chasen as she sat down at her vanity table and took off her wig, is beyond anyone's comprehension. After all, she is practically senile. It's always so embarrassing, particularly for the family, and, of course, so trying for the hostess.

Why don't they put her in a home? she asked herself, picking up her dressing gown from the bed. She could be well taken care of and be able to live there with her own kind until her time comes.

She stopped by her bathroom door and looked at herself in the full-length mirror. Throwing back her shoulders, she patted her stomach. Not bad, she thought. Staying young is purely a question of staying slim.

She opened the door and turned on the bathroom

light. Harold lay wide-eyed in the bathtub, his throat slashed, and blood dripping from his neck and wrists.

"My God! My God!" shrieked Mrs. Chasen. "Ohhh! Ohhh! This is too much. Too much!" She turned and fled crying down the hall.

Harold turned his head and listened. In the distance he could hear his mother's hysterical wailing. He looked at himself in the blood-streaked mirror and broke into a faint, satisfied smile.

"WE HAVE HAD SEVERAL SESSIONS now, Harold," Dr. Harley said, "but I don't think we can truthfully say there has been much progress. Would you agree?"

Harold, lying on the couch and staring at the ceiling, nodded in agreement.

"And why is that?"

Harold thought for a moment. "I don't know," he said.

Dr. Harley walked over to the window. "I think it is perhaps your reluctance to articulate or elaborate. We must communicate, Harold. Otherwise, I'll never understand. Now, let's go over these pretended suicides of yours once again. Since our last session your mother has reported three more. As I calculate, that makes a total of fifteen. Is that correct?"

Harold looked intently at the ceiling. "Yes," he

said, thoughtfully, "if you don't count the first one, and the time the bomb in the greenhouse exploded overnight."

Dr. Harley ran his hand over his thinning hair. "Fifteen," he said. "And they were all done for your mother's benefit?"

Harold considered that for a moment. "I wouldn't say 'benefit,'" he concluded.

"No," said Dr. Harley, "I suppose not." He sat at his desk. "But they were all designed to elicit a particular response from your mother, isn't that so? For example, the squashed-skull incident we talked about last time. You placed the dummy with the cantaloupe behind the rear wheel of your mother's car so that when she backed over it she thought she had run over your head. Now, the hysterics she displayed then would be the kind of thing you have been aiming for in these last three attempts. Am I right?"

"Well," said Harold. "That was one of the first. It was easier then."

"Uh, yes," said Dr. Harley. He leaned back in his chair. "Tell me about the bathroom incident last night."

"What do you want to know?"

"Would you rate it a success?"

Harold mulled that over. "It was the best response I've had in the last few weeks," he said.

"Did you leave a suicide note?"

"No. But I did write 'Farewell' on the mirror in blood. I don't think she saw it."

"Did you leave a suicide note for the hanging in the den?"

"Yes. I left it right on the desk. She didn't even pick it up."

"The hanging then was a failure?"

"Maybe it was the rigging," Harold mused. "Maybe I should have used a different harness."

"You seem to use very elaborate paraphernalia for these, uh, performances. The pool, for example. That must have taken a lot of work."

Harold took a deep breath. "Yes," he said with a slight smile of satisfaction. "It did. I had to build floats for the shoes and the suit. I even had to design a little oxygen device that lets you breathe underwater. It was a nice job."

"But not a success. At least, judging from what your mother told me."

Harold looked over at the doctor. "What did she say?" he asked.

"She said that she saw you floating in the swimming pool face down and fully clothed with a note saying 'Good-by World' pinned to your back. She told the maid to give you hot cocoa for lunch because she didn't want you to catch cold."

Harold looked back at the ceiling. It was a long time before he spoke. "It took me three days to set that up," he said finally.

Dr. Harley leaned forward in his chair. "Tell me, Harold," he said, changing the subject, "what do you do with your time?"

"You mean, when I'm not planning . . ."

"Yes. What is your daily activity? You don't go to school."

"No."

"And you don't go to work."

"No."

"So, how do you spend your day?"

Harold paused. "I go to junk yards."

"And what is your purpose in going there?"

Harold thought for a moment. "The junk," he said. "I like to look at junk."

"I see. What else do you do?"

"I like to watch the automobile crusher at the scrap-metal yard."

"And what else?"

"I like demolitions."

"You mean tearing down old buildings and things like that?"

"Yes, particularly with that great iron ball."

"That's very illuminating, Harold, and I think opens up several avenues for exploration in our next session. Right now your time is up. Give my best to your mother. I think I shall be seeing her early next week."

Harold got up off the couch and said good-by.

"Are you off to the junk yard?" Dr. Harley asked pleasantly.

"No," said Harold, "the cemetery."

The doctor was taken aback. "Oh—I'm sorry. Is it someone in the family?"

"No," said Harold as he opened the door, "I just like to go to funerals."

HAROLD STOOD ON THE EDGE of the crowd and listened to the minister say the final prayers. He preferred smaller funerals, he decided. With only a few people around the grave, the emotion seemed more intense. And, of course, with smaller funerals it was possible to get closer to the coffin and actually see it being lowered into the ground.

The minister droned on. The deceased must have been somebody important, he thought. This is quite a turnout. He looked around him and saw a little old lady not far off, seated under a tree. She looked like one of the mourners and Harold would have paid no attention to her, except that she was eating a slice of watermelon and spitting the seeds into a paper bag. He stared at her, more than a little puzzled. She seemed to be completely at ease, observing and enjoying everything around her, as if she were having a picnic in a neighborhood park. The minister's prayer drew to a close and Harold decided to leave. He took a final look at the old lady and concluded that she was definitely an odd one. Very weird, he said to himself, and climbed into his hearse and drove away.

"WHY YOU PURCHASED THAT monstrous black thing," said Mrs. Chasen at lunch, "is totally beyond me. You could have any car you want—a Porsche, a Jaguar, a nice little MG roadster. But no. We must have that eyesore parked in the driveway, an embarrassment to me and a shock to everyone else. I can't imagine what the ladies' auxiliary thought when they saw you—the son of their chairwoman—driving home in a hearse. Really, Harold, I don't know what to do. Drink up your milk, dear."

Harold drank his milk.

"It is not as if you were a stupid boy," continued Mrs. Chasen. "On the contrary, you have a very high IQ. So I simply do not understand this mortuary preoccupation. Where does it come from? Certainly not from me. I haven't the time for that kind of thinking.

From the minute I wake in the morning to the minute I go to bed at night, I am constantly on the move, doing things—committees, luncheons, the ballet—never an empty moment. But you, Harold, you never socialize, you never discuss, you never think about tomorrow. You merely fritter away your talents on those sanguine theatrical stunts—your little *divertissements*. There is no future in that, Harold. No matter how psychologically purging they may be. Your Uncle Victor suggests the Army. Well, perhaps you should go see him. I am certainly not fond of the Army, but maybe he can fathom you. After all, he was General MacArthur's right-hand man."

BRIGADIER GENERAL VICTOR E. BALL had in fact been General MacArthur's aide-de-camp for a short time in 1945. But in all fairness to MacArthur, he could hardly be said to have been the General's right-hand man, partly because he played no role in any command decision, but mainly because he had no right hand. Indeed, he had no right arm, as it had been shot off during training maneuvers at Fort Jackson, South Carolina. Normally an officer would be expected to retire after such a distinction, but General Ball was not the type of man who gave up without a fight. As he saw it, the biggest handicap in the Army brought about by the lack of a right arm was the inability to salute in the required military fashion. After some experimentation he devised a mechanical device that lay folded in his empty sleeve. When he pulled the cord of his *fourragère* with his left hand, the sleeve sprang up to his forehead, delivering a snappy West Point salute. With this device, and the influence of several friends in the Pentagon, General Ball was able to make the Army his career. As he said to his nephew:

"The Army is not only my home, Harold, it is my life. And it could be your life too. I know how your mother feels. She insists I hold on to your draft records, but if it were up to me I'd process your file and have you shipped off to basic tomorrow. Believe me—you'd have a grand time."

The general stood up from his desk and gestured at the military posters hung on his office walls. "Take a look about you, Harold," he said. "There's the Army drubbing the Spicks at San Juan, clobbering the Chinks, whipping the redskins, and battling its way across the Remagen bridge. Ah, it's a great life. It offers history and education. Action. Adventure. Advising! You'll see war—firsthand! And plenty of slant-eyed girls. Why, it will make a man out of you, Harold. You put on the uniform and you walk tall—a glint in your eye, a spring in your step, and the knowledge in your heart that you are fighting for peace. And serving your country."

He stopped before a portrait of Nathan Hale with a noose about his neck.

"Just like Nathan Hale," he said. He pulled his lanyard and his sleeve snapped up a salute. "That's what this country needs—more Nathan Hales." He paused at attention in front of the portrait before he let his sleeve fall neatly back in place.

"And do you know what?" said the general, turning to Harold, seated by the window.

"What?" said Harold.

The general stood in front of him and confidentially bent down. "I think," he whispered slowly, "I think I see a little Nathan Hale in you."

Harold stared blankly back at his uncle.

The general smiled and punched him on the shoulder. "Think about it," he said and walked back to his desk.

HAROLD'S DECAPITATED HEAD stood upright on the silver serving platter while Harold placed sprigs of parsley in the blood around the neck. When he heard his mother coming down the stairs, he quickly placed the large silver cover over the serving dish and put it under the table. He left the dining room to meet her in the hall.

"Harold, dear, I have only a few minutes but I want to inform you of my decision. Please sit down."

Harold sat down and Mrs. Chasen started to put on her long white gloves.

"Harold," she said matter-of-factly, "it is time for you to begin thinking of your future. You are nineteen, almost twenty. You have led an idle, happy, carefree life up to the present—the life of a child. But it is now time to put away childish things and take on adult responsibilities. We would all like to sail through life with no thought of tomorrow. But that cannot be. We have our duty. Our obligations. Our principles. In short," said Mrs. Chasen, finishing with her gloves, "I think it is time you got married."

"What?" said Harold.

"Married," said Mrs. Chasen, picking up her evening purse and going to the door. "We are going to find you a girl so you can get married."

HAROLD KNELT IN THE CHURCH and listened to the organ playing softly. He looked above the altar at the large stained-glass window showing St. Thomas Aquinas writing in a book with a feather. Thomas Aquinas never got married, thought Harold, and glanced over at the man in the open coffin. I wonder if *he* ever did. I wonder who he was, anyway.

Silver-haired Father Finnegan stepped up to the pulpit and scanned the few isolated mourners before him. He opened his book and read as he had done countless times before.

"And so dear brethren let us pray to the Lord, King of Glory, that He may bless and deliver all souls of the faithful departed from the pains of hell and the bottomless pit, deliver them from the lion's mouth and the darkness therein, but rather bring them to the bliss of heaven, the holy light, and eternal rest."

As Father Finnegan continued his weary prayer, Harold, kneeling near the back of the church, quietly sat up. He looked over at a portrait of the sorrowing Madonna.

"Psst!"

Harold listened.

"Psssst!"

Harold turned around. Across the aisle three rows back a white-haired old lady smiled and gaily waved at him. Harold turned back. That was the woman at the cemetery, he said to himself, the one eating watermelon. What does she want with me?

"PSSSST!"

Harold started and turned. The old lady had moved. She now knelt right behind him. She grinned.

"Like some licorice?" she asked sweetly, offering him a little bag. She spoke with a slight European accent.

"Uh, no. Thank you," whispered Harold and knelt down.

"You're welcome," she whispered back.

Keeping his eyes on the altar, Harold listened intently. After a few minutes he heard the old lady get up noisily from her pew, genuflect, walk into his pew, and kneel beside him. She gave him a friendly jab.

"Did you know him?" she asked, gesturing at the deceased.

"Uh, no," whispered Harold, trying to appear involved in the service.

"Neither did I," said the old lady brightly. "I heard he was eighty years old. I'll be eighty next week. A good time to move on, don't you think?"

"I don't know," said Harold, standing up with the rest of the congregation. Father Finnegan blessed the coffin and the pallbearers wheeled it out.

"I mean seventy-five is too early," the old lady continued, standing beside him, "but at eighty-five, well, you're just marking time and you may as well look over the horizon."

The few mourners filed out of the church. Harold felt a tug on his sleeve.

"Look at them," she whispered loudly to him. "I've never understood this mania for black. I mean no one sends black flowers, do they? Black flowers are dead flowers, and who would send dead flowers to a funeral?" She laughed. "How absurd," she said. "It's change. It's all change."

Harold walked out of the pew and the old lady followed.

"What do you think of old fat Tom?" she asked.

"Who?" said Harold.

"St. Thomas Aquinas up there. I saw you looking at him."

"I think he's . . . uh . . . a great thinker."

"Oh, yes. But a little old-fashioned, don't you think? Like roast swan. Oh, dear! Look at her."

They stopped before the dour portrait of the Madonna.

"May I borrow this?" she said, taking the felt pen from Harold's coat pocket. With a few deft strokes she drew a cheery smile on the Virgin's mouth.

Harold looked about the empty church to see if anyone was watching.

"There. That's better," the old lady said. "They never give the poor thing a chance to laugh. Heaven knows she has a lot to be happy about. In fact," she added, looking at several statues at the back of the church, "they all have a lot to be happy about. Excuse me."

Harold made a halfhearted gesture for his pen but to no avail. The old lady was already in the back of the church, drawing smiles on St. Joseph, St. Anthony, and St. Theresa.

"An unhappy saint is a contradiction in terms," she explained.

"Uh, yes," said Harold nervously.

"And why do they go on about that?" she asked.

Harold looked over at a crucifix.

"You'd think," she said, walking out the door, "that no one ever read the end of the story."

Harold followed her out to the street.

"Uh, could I have my pen back now please?" he asked.

"Oh, of course," she said, giving it to him. "What is your name?"

"Harold Chasen."

"How do you do?" She smiled. "I am the Countess Mathilda Chardin, but you may call me Maude." When she smiled, the lines around her eyes made them seem even more sparkling and blue.

Harold politely offered his hand. "Nice to meet you," he said.

She shook his hand. "I think we shall be great friends, don't you?" She took a large ring of keys from her purse and opened the door of the car at the curb.

"Can I drop you anywhere, Harold?" she asked.

"No," answered Harold quickly. "Thank you. I have my car."

"Well then, I must be off. We shall have to meet again."

Inside the church Father Finnegan stood dumbfounded before the beaming statues.

Maude raced the motor and released the brake.

"Harold," she called, "do you dance?"

"What?"

"Do you sing and dance?"

"Uh, no."

"No." She smiled sadly. "I thought not." She stepped on the gas. With a great screech of burning rubber, the car flew from the curb, tore down the street, and spun around a distant corner. One could still hear the gears shifting in the distance.

Harold stared after it in wonderment.

Father Finnegan, who was standing at the church door, had also seen it depart. "That woman—" he said to no one in particular, "she took my car."

MRS. CHASEN SAT AT THE DESK in the den and spoke to her son standing opposite her. "I have here, Harold, the forms sent out by the National Computer Dating Service," she said. "It seems to me that since you do not get along with the daughters of any of my friends, this is the best way for you to find a prospective wife."

Harold opened his mouth but his mother waved any objection aside.

"Please, Harold," she said. "Sit down. We have a lot to do and I have to be at the dressmaker's at three." She looked over the papers.

"The Computer Dating Service offers you at least three dates on the initial investment. They say they screen out the fat and ugly, so it is obviously a firm of high standards. I'm sure they can find you at least one girl who is compatible."

Harold drew over a chair and sat down.

"Now first, here is the personality interview, which you are to fill out and return. There are fifty questions with five possible responses to check: A—Absolutely Yes, B—Yes, C—Not Sure, D—No, and E—Absolutely No. Are you ready, Harold?"

Harold looked at his mother with his mournful brown eyes.

"The first question is: Are you uncomfortable meeting new people? Well, I think that's a 'yes.' Don't you agree, Harold? Even an 'absolutely yes.' We'll put down 'A' on that. Number two: Should sex education be taught outside the home? I would say no, wouldn't you, Harold? We'll give a 'D' there. Three: Do you enjoy spending a lot of time by yourself? Well, that's easy, isn't it? Absolutely yes. Mark 'A.' Should women run for President of the United States? I don't see why not. Absolutely yes. Do you often invite friends to your home? No, you never do, Harold. Absolutely no. Do you often get the feeling that perhaps life isn't worth living? Hmmm."

Mrs. Chasen glanced up. "What would you say, Harold?"

Harold gazed stoically at his mother.

"You think 'A'? Or 'B'?"

He blinked.

"Well, let's put down 'C'—not sure. Seven: Is the subject of sex being overexploited by our mass media? That would have to be 'yes,' wouldn't it? Do judges favor some lawyers? Yes, I suppose they do. Is it acceptable for a schoolteacher to smoke or drink in public? . . ."

As Mrs. Chasen rattled on, Harold slowly opened his coat and took out a small gun. Reaching into his side pocket, he brought out six bullets and, while his mother filled out the questionnaire, he carefully and deliberately loaded each bullet into the chamber.

"Do you sometimes have headaches or backaches after a difficult day? Yes, I do indeed. Do you go to sleep easily? I'd say so. Do you believe in capital punishment for murder? Oh, yes. Do you believe churches have a strong influence to upgrade the general morality? Yes, again. In your opinion are social affairs usually a waste of time? Heavens, no! Can God influence our lives? Yes. Absolutely yes. Have you ever crossed the street to avoid meeting someone? Well, I'm sure you have, haven't you, dear? . . ."

Harold inserted the last bullet and snapped the chamber shut. He looked up at his mother. She was too absorbed to hear anything. He pulled back the hammer, cocking the gun. Still she read on.

"Did you enjoy life as a child? Oh, yes." She sighed, turning the page and continuing, "You were a wonderful baby, Harold."

He slowly raised the gun until it was pointing directly at her head.

"Does your personal religion or philosophy include a life after death? Oh, yes, indeed. That's absolutely. Do you have ups and downs without obvious reasons? You do, don't you, dear? Mark 'A.'"

Harold watched and listened. Slowly he turned the gun around until he was looking straight down the barrel.

"Do you remember jokes and take pleasure relating them to others? You don't, do you, dear? Mark 'E.'"

Gradually he tightened his finger around the trigger.

"Do you think the sexual revolution has gone too far? It certainly seems to have. Should evolution—"

With a loud blast the gun fired, knocking him backwards out of the chair onto the floor. He lay there lifelessly as blood trickled from the neat round hole in his forehead.

Mrs. Chasen looked up.

"Harold," she said impatiently. "Harold, please! Did you hear me? Should evolution be taught in our public schools?"

"I DON'T THINK I'M GETTING THROUGH to Mother like I used to," Harold confided to Dr. Harley later that day.

"Oh?" said the doctor.

Harold brooded briefly. "I think I'm losing my touch."

DARK GRAY CLOUDS ROLLED IN from the coast and the wind rustled the trees at the cemetery. Father Finnegan glanced up from the burial service and decided that it looked like rain. He skipped the holy water and began the final prayers.

Harold looked about the small group of mourners. Some put up their umbrellas and huddled beneath them. Others stood silently, their hats in their hands.

"Psst!"

Harold turned.

Across the grave, Maude, outfitted in a yellow raincoat and matching sou'wester, waved her hand to catch his attention.

Embarrassed, he quickly gazed down at the coffin, pretending he hadn't seen her.

"Psst!"

He didn't move.

"PSSSST!"

He looked up.

She gave him a big smile and winked.

He nodded slightly.

Father Finnegan closed his book and, mumbling the last blessing, noticed Maude. For a moment he thought he recognized her, but before he was certain she seemed to be overcome by grief and disappeared behind some people.

He looked over at Harold. Harold looked down at the coffin. Father Finnegan concluded the prayer.

The mourners responded "Amen," blessed themselves, and hurried to their cars.

"A moment, please," said Father Finnegan, catching up to Harold. "You're the Chasen boy, aren't you?"

"Uh, yes," answered Harold.

"Tell me, who was that old lady you were waving at earlier?"

"I wasn't waving at her. She was waving at me."

Just then Maude drove by in Harold's hearse and stopped. She leaned out the window.

"Can I give you a lift, Harold?" she asked.

Harold was struck dumb. Father Finnegan walked around to the window.

"Excuse me, madam," he said, "but are you not the lady who drove my car off yesterday?"

"Was that the one with the St. Christopher medal on the dashboard?"

"Yes."

"Then I suppose it was me. Hop in, Harold."

Harold decided not to ask for explanations. He opened the door and got in.

"But where is it?" asked Father Finnegan, becoming a little perturbed.

"Where's what?" asked Maude.

"My car. Where did you leave it?"

"Oh, that. I think perhaps at the orphanage. No, it's not, because I still had it at the African Arts Center. Ever been there, Father? Oh, you'll enjoy it. They have the most colorful carvings. Primitive, of course, but some quite erotic."

Realization hit Father Finnegan. "You painted the statues," he said.

"Oh, yes," said Maude brightly. "How did you like them?"

"Well, that's the point. I didn't."

"Don't be too discouraged," she said, releasing the brake. "Aesthetic appreciation always takes a little time. Bye-bye."

"Wait!" said Father Finnegan, but his voice was lost in the screeching of tires and a roar of exhaust as Maude sped off in the hearse and turned the corner.

Harold picked himself off the floor and looked out of the window. The gravestones merged together in a flickering blur of gray. Maude came to the entrance of the cemetery and spun out onto the main road. Cruising at about sixty miles an hour, she settled back and relaxed.

"What a delight it is, Harold," she said, "to bump into you again. I knew we were going to be great friends the moment I saw you. You go to funerals often, don't you?"

Harold had one hand braced on the dashboard and the other on the back of the seat. "Yes," he answered, without taking his eyes off the road.

"Oh, so do I. They're such fun, aren't they? It's all change. All revolving. Burials and births. The end to the beginning, the beginning to the end. The great circle of life."

She made a sudden left-hand turn that sent a terrified Volkswagen into a heart-stopping change of lanes. "My, this old thing handles well. Ever drive a hearse, Harold?"

Harold swallowed. "Yes," he said hoarsely.

"Well, it's a new experience for me."

She raced over a small hill, causing Harold's head to bounce repeatedly on the ceiling, and then made another sudden left-hand turn that threw the rear wheels into a momentary slide.

"Not too good on curves," she exclaimed, and put her foot down on the gas. "Shall I take you home, Harold?"

Harold, halfway between the seat and the floor, blurted out faintly, "But this is my car."

"Your hearse?"

"Yearse!"

Maude stepped on the brakes and skidded to a dusty halt in the gravel by the side of the road. She looked over at him. "Fancy that," she cooed. "My, my. Then you shall take me home."

HAROLD DROVE SLOWLY and carefully as he listened to Maude elaborate on her system of acquiring cars.

"After his release from the penitentiary, Big Sweeney began work in a printing shop, where I met him and we became friends. Then when he received 'the call' and left for the monastery in Tibet, he gave his collection of keys to me, as a present. Wasn't that nice? Of course, I've had to make some additions for the newer models, but not as many as you might think. Once you have your basic set, it's only a question of variation."

"Do you mean with that ring of keys you get into any car you want and just drive off?"

"Not *any* car. I like to keep a variety. I'm always looking for the new experience, like this one. I liked it."

"Thank you."

"You're welcome. Oh, there's my house over there."

Harold pulled the hearse over and stopped before a clapboard cottage with a walnut tree in the front yard. Several other old houses stood nearby on spacious lots, some with barns or stables in the back, but across the street and on down the hill the land had been subdivided. The houses there looked very much alike, all small, boxlike, and crowded together.

"Looks as if the weather has cleared up," said Maude, getting out of the hearse. Harold closed her door. He was still troubled.

"But when you take these cars," he asked, "don't you think you are . . . well, wronging the owners?"

"What owners, Harold? We don't *own* anything. It's a transitory world. We come on the earth with nothing, and we go out with nothing, so isn't *ownership* a little absurd? I wonder if the post has come."

She opened up a wooden box on the porch and took out the mail.

"Oh, look. More books. I just sign their cards and they keep sending them to me. I received an encyclopedia in Dutch last week. Here, hold them, Harold, would you please?"

Harold took the books while Maude glanced through her letters.

"Very odd, too," she said, "because I don't speak Dutch. German, French, English, some Spanish, some

29

Italian, and a little Japanese. But no Dutch. Of course, that's nothing against the Dutch. I thought Queen Wilhelmina was a wonderful woman. Come inside, Harold. I'll look at these later."

Harold walked into the house and put the books down on a table.

"About those keys," he persisted, as Maude hung up her hat and coat. "I still think you upset people when they find their car is gone, and I'm not sure that is right."

"Well," she answered, "if some people are upset because they feel they have a hold on some things, then I'm merely acting as a gentle reminder. I'm sort of breaking it easy. Here today, gone tomorrow, so don't get attached to *things*. Now, with that in mind, I'm not against collecting stuff. Why, look around you. I've collected quite a lot of stuff in my time."

Harold looked around the large living room and was struck by the odd assortment of furnishings. No two chairs were alike. The couch was covered with a Persian rug. Colorful canvases hung on the walls, a baby grand piano stood in one corner next to a huge carving of highly polished wood, and a samovar full of dried flowers sat on a tapa mat by the fireplace near some Japanese screens.

"It's very . . . interesting," said Harold, somewhat at a loss for words. "Very different."

"Oh, it's all foolish memorabilia," said Maude, going over to the window. "Incidental but not integral, if you know what I mean. Oh, come look. The birds."

She opened the window and filled a small tin cup with seed. Then she released a spring that shot the cup out along a wire and dumped the seed on a bird table. Harold was impressed with the mechanical ingenuity of the device.

"Isn't that delightful?" said Maude. "This is my daily ritual. I love them so much. The only wild life I see any more. Look at them. Free as a bird."

She took the empty birdseed box into the kitchen. "At one time I used to break into pet shops and liberate the canaries, but I gave it up as an idea before its time. The zoos are full and the prisons overflowing. My, my. How the world so dearly loves a cage."

She looked out the window over the sink. "Look, Harold. There's Madame Arouet cultivating her garden. Yoo-hoo!"

She waved at the black-clad old woman diligently hoeing in her large vegetable patch, but the old woman didn't notice.

Maude sighed. "She's really very sweet. But so old-fashioned. Please sit down, Harold. I'll put on the kettle and we'll have a nice hot cup of tea."

"Thank you," said Harold. "But I really have to go."

"It's oat straw tea. You've never had oat straw tea, have you?"

"No."

"Well then." She smiled and picked up the kettle.

"No, really. Thank you, but it's an appointment I shouldn't miss."

"Oh, at the dentist's."

"Sort of."

"Well then, you must come back and visit."

"All right," said Harold and walked to the door.

"My door is always open."

"All right."

"See you soon."

"Okay."

"Promise?"

Harold turned. "I promise," he said, and smiled.

DR. HARLEY'S OFFICE CEILING was plastered and painted white. To the casual observer, thought Harold, it would look smooth, flat, and uninteresting.

"Harold."

But to a searching eye and over a period of time, the craftsmanship of the painter and plasterer became visibly apparent, so that what had once seemed dull and ordinary became fascinatingly impressionistic.

"Harold."

A layer of plaster became a craggy desert of light and shade, and a swirl of paint evoked the swell of a polar sea.

"You don't seem to be listening, Harold. I asked you, do you have any friends?"

Harold abandoned his musings and concentrated on the question. "No," he answered.

"None at all?"

Harold considered. "Well, maybe one."

"Would you care to talk about this friend?"

"No."

"Does your mother know this friend?"

"No."

"Is this a friend you had when you were away at school?"

"No."

"I see." Dr. Harley ran his hand over the back of his head. He decided on a new tack.

"Were you happy at school?" he asked.

"Yes."

"You liked your teachers?"

"Yes."

"Your classmates?"

"Yes."

"Your studies?"

"Yes."

"Then why did you leave?"

"I burned down the chemistry building."

Dr. Harley stood up slowly and walked to the window. He adjusted the Venetian blind.

"We are not relating today, Harold," he said. "I sense a definite lack of participation on your part. We are not *communicating*. Now, I find you a very interesting case, Harold, one with which I would like to continue, but this reluctance to commit yourself is detrimental to the psychoanalytical process and can only hinder the possibility of effective treatment. Do you understand?"

"Yes," said Harold.

"Very well," said Dr. Harley.

He sat down.

"Tell me, Harold," he began after a pause. "Do you remember your father at all?"

"No," said Harold, and added, "I'd have liked to."

"Really. Why?"

"I'd have liked to talk to him."

"What would you say?"

"I'm not sure. I'd show him my hearse, and my stuff."

"What stuff?"

"All the stuff in my room—my workbench, my chemistry set, my rope harness for hangings, my oxygen device for drownings, my poster of *The Phantom of the Opera*—I have a lot of things."

"They sound intriguing."

"Well," said Harold thoughtfully, "they're incidental but not integral, if you know what I mean."

HAROLD BROUGHT THE SILVER serving dish into his room and placed it on the workbench. He took the cover off and looked at his severed head, sitting in a pool of dried blood garnished with sprigs of parsley. It was certainly a good likeness, he decided, and it might have worked a month or two ago, but right now the whole idea was a little too obvious. He picked up the head and peeled off the latex blood. The plan was to have had it served as part of the cold buffet, when his mother and her guests returned from the benefit performance of *Salome*, but, as all military strategists know, he said to himself, even the best plan will fail if the tactics become too familiar to the enemy.

He took the head and placed it on the neck of the mannequin, sitting fully clothed on the edge of his bed. The head did not fit perfectly, as the peg in the dummy's neck was too loose. Harold went into his closet and looked among the shelves for his box of tools. He picked up a meat cleaver, but he couldn't find a chisel or a screwdriver.

Mrs. Chasen knocked on the door and came into the room. She wore an evening gown, had a fur wrap over her arm, and held in her hand several IBM cards.

"Now, listen, Harold," she said, addressing the dummy on the edge of the bed. "I have here the cards of the three girls sent out by the Computer Dating Service."

Harold stopped his search. He listened, puzzled, standing in the closet with the meat cleaver in his hand.

"I've telephoned the girls and invited each of them to have lunch with us before you take them out. The first one is coming tomorrow at one thirty. We'll chat in the library and serve luncheon at two. Have you got that?"

Harold looked at his mother through the crack in the closet door. She continued to address the dummy.

"Above all, Harold, I expect you to act like a gentleman. Remember your manners and try to make this girl feel at home. Well, I'm off to the opera with the Fergusons," she said, putting on her wrap. "I only hope they can maneuver around that great black thing of yours in the driveway. You realize that, if your garage wasn't full of auto parts and other junk, you could park it there."

She went to the door. "Look, Harold, I'm leaving the IBM cards here." She placed them on a table next to a gallon of Max Factor blood. "Good heavens." She sighed, looking at the bottle. "I don't know. Whatever became of model airplanes?"

The front doorbell rang downstairs.

"That's them," she said, turning. I'll . . ." She paused and looked intently at the dummy.

"You look a little pale, dear," she said. "You get a good night's sleep. After all, you want to look your best for tomorrow."

She left, closing the door behind her.

Harold walked out of the closet and went over to the dummy. He looked at it carefully. He shook his head and went back to the closet to continue the search for his box of tools.

THE NEXT DAY AT ONE THIRTY-FIVE Mrs. Chasen went to the front door and greeted the first computer date, a cute, blonde, pug-nosed little coed called Candy Gulf.

"Hello," she said. "I'm Candy Gulf."

"How do you do?" said Mrs. Chasen. "Won't you come in?"

"Oh, thank you."

"Harold is out in the garden. He'll be in in a moment. Shall we go into the library?"

"Oh, all right."

"I understand you are at the university, Candy," said Mrs. Chasen as they walked down the hall.

"Yes, I am."

"And what are you studying?"

"Poli Sci. With a Home Ec minor."

"Uh, Polly Sigh?"

"Political Science. It's all about what's going on."

"Oh, I see," said Mrs. Chasen, ushering her into the library.

"Look. There's Harold out the window." She waved at Harold as he walked across the lawn.

Candy waved too. Harold saw them and waved back. Then he walked behind the gardener's shed.

"He seems very nice," said Candy.

"*I* think he is," said Mrs. Chasen pleasantly. "Please sit down."

Candy seated herself facing Mrs. Chasen, who sat with her back to the French windows.

"Is Harold interested in what's going on?" Candy asked. "I mean, I think it's such a super thing to study. And then, of course, I can always fall back on Home Ec. That's Home Economics."

"Yes," said Mrs. Chasen a little vaguely. "That's good planning."

"Well, it's my life."

"Tell me, Candy, are you a regular in this computer club?"

"Heavens, no!" she answered and giggled. Glancing out the window she saw Harold come from behind the gardener's shed with a large can marked "Kerosene."

"I don't have to worry about dates," she went on. "You see, the other girls in my sorority, well, we decided that somebody should try it. So, we drew straws and I lost!" She giggled again, then quickly added, "But I am looking forward to meeting Harold."

Mrs. Chasen smiled. Behind her on the lawn Harold was pouring the contents of the can all over himself. Candy looked at him a little nonplused.

"I think I should mention, Candy," said Mrs. Chasen, "that Harold does have his eccentric moments."

"Oh, *yes!*" said Candy, finally comprehending. "That's all right. I've got a brother who's a real cutup too."

And she giggled to show her good sportsmanship.

"Do you know, I'll never forget the time we had this old TV set with no parts in it. Well, Tommy stuck his head behind it and started giving a newscast before the whole family. We were all hysterical. And here's little Tommy pretending to be Walter Cronkite."

She looked out the window and her mouth fell open. Harold was a mass of flames.

"Yes," said Mrs. Chasen, "I'm sure it must have been very funny."

Candy jumped up and pointed at the window. "Har . . . Har . . . Harold!" she screamed.

Mrs. Chasen looked at her, a trifle concerned. "Yes, dear," she said. "Why, here's Harold now."

Harold walked in and nodded a greeting.

Candy's eyes popped. Her whole body went slack.

"Harold, dear, I'd like you to meet Candy Gulf."

Harold offered his hand.

Suddenly Candy began to sob convulsively. She covered her face with her hands and continued crying until Mrs. Chasen called a cab for her.

"I don't understand it," said Mrs. Chasen as they watched the cab drive off. "It was something to do with a story about Walter Cronkite."

THE NEXT MORNING Harold knocked on Maude's door. The latch was missing and the door swung open.

"Anyone home?" he cried, walking into the living room.

No answer.

"Maude?" he called.

Silence.

He glanced around the room and inspected some of the things that caught his eye.

Over the fireplace a furled beige umbrella hung like an old trophy. Its bone handle was shaped like the head of a goose, but one of the inlaid eyes was missing, making the goose look as if he were winking.

He walked over to the Japanese screens. Behind them was an eating alcove built in the Japanese manner—a raised platform covered with *tatami* matting. Strands of acorns and small sea shells hung across the bedroom doorway. He separated them and glanced briefly at the ornately carved and canopied bed inside. It looks like something from *Lohengrin*, he said to himself with a smile and walked over to the windows.

An old Victrola with a stack of gramophone records stood along the wall. Beside it sat an old TV console with its picture tube removed. The cabinet was used as the shelf for a microscope, and the top served as the stand for a telescope that peered upward out the open window.

By the couch in the middle of the room a strange boxlike machine sat on a table. Harold looked at it intently but he could not make out what it was. The lights and switches and the rack of brightly colored metal cylinders puzzled him, nor did he understand the word "Odorific" that was floridly lettered on its side.

He walked to the piano and examined the odd assortment of silver frames that stood on top of it. Here was another puzzle. All the frames were empty. They contained neither picture nor photograph.

Harold shrugged and stood for a moment before the big wooden sculpture. The lacquer shone in the morning light, making the grain seem almost like liquid, flowing through and around the curves and holes. Instinctively he reached out to run his hand along the smooth surfaces, but stopped short, deciding he shouldn't. He turned and walked out to the kitchen.

Through the window he saw Madame Arouet working in her garden, and he went outside to talk to her.

"Excuse me," he said. "Have you seen Maude?"

She stopped her hoeing and looked up at him from beneath her wide straw hat. Her wrinkled face showed a weary resignation, but her dark, watery eyes questioned him keenly.

"Maude," said Harold. "Do you know where she is?"

"Maude?" murmured Madame Arouet in a heavy French accent. She didn't understand.

"Yes," said Harold. "Maude."

"Ah! Maude!" She pointed to a large barnlike building farther up the hill.

"Thank you," said Harold and started off. "Thank you. *Merci*."

Madame Arouet bobbed her head and watched him go. A strange sadness filled her face. She turned back to hoeing her turnips.

Harold arrived at the building and knocked on the

door. It was too thick to hear through, so he opened it up and stepped inside. The first thing he saw was an enormous block of ice in the center of the room, with a wire-haired little man on a platform beside it energetically chipping away. All around were the trappings of a sculptor's studio—some hanging draperies, some old furniture, some plaster casts and molds. But what struck Harold was the abundance of tools, not only hammers and chisels but winches and wrenches and power saws.

"Excuse me," he said, and then he noticed that the old man was trying to shape a female figure from the ice and kept looking over at his live model, posing like Venus. Harold could see her outline through the ice. She was naked. He hastily turned to go.

"What do you want?" asked the sculptor, stopping his work.

"It's all right. I was just looking for Maude."

The nude model poked her head around from behind the ice.

"Harold?" she said happily.

"*Maude???!*"

BACK IN HER KITCHEN, Maude filled the kettle and placed it on the stove. Harold sat in the living room, brooding.

43

"There we are," said Maude. "It will be ready in a minute. By the way, Harold, how's your hearse?"

"Oh, it's fine."

"She seemed yare to me." Maude brought in a tray of tea things and began setting the table.

"Excuse the mismatched saucers," she said.

Harold sat back on the couch. "Do you often model for Glaucus?" he asked nonchalantly.

"Heavens, no!" said Maude. "I don't have the time. But I do like to keep in practice, and poor Glaucus occasionally needs to have his memory refreshed as to the contours of the female form."

She finished with the table and looked at him squarely.

"Do you disapprove?" she asked.

"Me? No!" said Harold and crossed his legs. "Of course not."

Maude smiled. "Really? Do you think it's wrong?"

Harold looked up at her. She wanted the truth. He mulled it over. Is it wrong? he asked himself.

"No," he answered simply, and smiled.

Maude smiled back. "Oh, I'm so happy you said that, Harold, because I want to show you my paintings. Come over here. I call this 'The Rape of Rome.' What do you think?"

Harold looked at the large canvas. Vaguely Rubensesque and full of fire and movement, it depicted a bevy of fat pink ladies struggling with their clothes, their abductors, and a couple of rearing steeds.

"I like it," he said.

"And, of course, down here is quite a graphic depiction of Leda and the Swan."

Harold looked at the corner of the painting.

"Why that's . . ."

"Yes," said Maude coyly. "I thought it called for a self-portrait. Now, over here is my favorite. It's called 'Rainbow with Egg Underneath and an Elephant.' What does that do for your eyes?"

"It's very colorful. Very . . . full."

"Thank you. It was my last. I then became infatuated with these—my 'odorifics.'"

She went over to the boxlike machine and attached a small hose with a sort of oxygen mask at its end.

"Ever heard of these, Harold? Of course, this one I built myself. A young Sioux in a commune gave me the basic blueprint. Here, hold this."

Harold held the mask while Maude fidgeted with the dials and pump.

"Have you noticed that art ignores the nose?" she said. "It's true. So I said let's give the old *schnauze* a treat. Have a kind of olfactory banquet. I began first on the easiest—roast beef, old books, mown grass— then I went on to these." She picked up the metal cylinders and read off their titles: "'An Evening at

Maxims,' 'Mexican Farmyard.' Here's one you'd like, 'Snowfall on Forty-second Street.'"

She took the cylinder and screwed it into the box. Then she helped Harold adjust the mask over his nose.

"Ready?" she said and threw the switch. The lights went on and the pistons began to pump. "Okay. What do you smell?"

Harold closed his eyes and breathed in slowly.

"Subways," he said surprisedly.

Maude grinned. "Go on."

"Perfume . . . cigarettes . . . cologne . . ." He became more and more excited. "Carpet . . . roasting chestnuts. . . . *Snow!*"

"Oh, yes." Maude laughed and turned it off. "You can put together any number of them."

"That's really great," said Harold. He put the mask down on the table. "I wonder if I could make one. I'm pretty good with machines."

"Oh, sure you could. I'll give it to you and you can see how it works. It's very simple. You could probably improve on it. I thought, myself, of continuing—graduating to the abstract and free-smelling—but then I decided to switch to the tactile." She pointed to the wooden sculpture. "That's my *chef d'oeuvre*."

"Yes. It looks great."

"No," said Maude. "You have to touch it." She demonstrated. "You have to run your hands over it, get closer to it, really reach out, and *feel*. Go ahead. You try it."

Harold gingerly touched the wood and ran his hand over a sensuous curve.

"That's right. How's the sensation?"

The kettle whistled from the kitchen.

"Oh, excuse me," said Maude. "I'll get the tea. Go ahead now, Harold. Stroke, palm, caress, *explore*."

Harold watched her disappear behind the kitchen door. He turned back to the sculpture and put both hands firmly on its smooth surfaces. He stepped closer, and as he moved his hands he found himself enjoying the feel of the polished wood. His hands became more daring. They swept around a large hole and for a moment he felt the odd compulsion to stick his head inside it. He controlled the impulse, but it refused to go away. He looked over his shoulder at the kitchen. Maude was humming behind the door. His hands continued outlining the opening and suddenly he stuck his head in it, quickly pulled it out, and took two steps back from the sculpture. He looked around. Maude was still humming in the kitchen. No one had seen him. He relaxed, clapped his hands together, and smiled.

Maude brought in the tea. "Here we are," she said. "Oat straw tea and ginger pie. Sit down, Harold."

"This is certainly a new experience for me," he said, holding Maude's chair for her before he sat down.

"Oh, thank you, Harold. Well, try something new each day, that's my motto. After all, we're given life to find it out. It doesn't last forever."

"You look as if you could."

"Me? Ha! Did I tell you I'll be eighty on Saturday?"

"You don't look eighty."

"That's the influence of the right food, the right exercise, and the right breathing. Greet the dawn with 'The Breath of Fire.'"

She sat back in her chair and demonstrated "The Breath of Fire," followed by "The Bellows." They left her a little winded.

"Of course," she said, laughing and catching her breath, "there's no doubt the body is giving out. I'm well into autumn. I'll have to be giving it all up after Saturday."

She finished pouring the tea and put down the pot.

"That's an old teapot," remarked Harold.

"Sterling silver," said Maude wistfully. "It was my dear mother-in-law's, part of a dinner set of fifty pieces. It was sent to me, one of the few things that survived." Her voice trailed off and she absently sipped her tea.

Harold regarded her quizzically. She seemed suddenly far away.

"The ginger pie is delicious," he said, breaking the silence.

Maude looked up. "What? Oh, thank you, Harold. I'm glad you like it. It's my own recipe. I'll give it to you if you like."

"Oh, I don't cook."

"Why not?"

"Because I . . . well, men don't . . . I mean . . ." He paused. "I don't know why," he said.

"Oh, it's fun. Try a cake. It's like making a collage from old magazine pictures. You have your ingredients, you throw them together, and presto! You've created something new, something different. Suddenly you're a somebody. You've made a cake."

"And you get to eat it," said Harold.

"Of course," said Maude. "You get to eat it. You even get to share it. I'm all for everybody baking cakes. But enough of me. Tell me about yourself. What do you do, Harold, when you aren't visiting funerals?"

"Oh, a lot of things," said Harold, smiling.

"Like what?"

"Well, I'll show you."

HAROLD AND MAUDE sat on the hood of Harold's hearse and watched a construction company across the street tear down an old building. A huge crane swung a heavy lead ball crashing through the brick and mortar, and a giant bulldozer shoveled up the debris and dumped it into a truck.

"Fascinating," said Maude over the din. "Fascinating," and she continued to gaze, enraptured.

"Thanks," said Harold. "I've got another place too."

Seated on a hill near the junk yard, they saw car after car being picked up by a monstrous claw and dropped into a crusher where, after a noisy pounding, they were shuffled out as twisted little bales of scrap.

"There is definitely a certain attraction," said Maude, summing it up. "No question. It's all very thrilling." She took a bite of a raw carrot. "But I ask you, Harold," she said, munching solemnly. "Is it enough?"

"What do you mean?"

Maude smiled. "Come. I'll show you."

They drove to a large vegetable field near the sea and knelt between the rows of early cabbages.

"I love to watch things grow," Maude said. "Cast your eyes on those little rascals, Harold. The last time I was here they were just cracking the soil and pushing up their tiny green heads. Now look at them. Look at the new leaves inside."

"Yes, I see," said Harold eagerly. "They're all curled up and fragile—like a baby's hand."

"We ought to go see some babies too."

"What?"

"We ought to go visit a maternity ward. Have you ever been in one?"

"No, I guess I never have."

"Oh, they're lots of fun. Maybe we can go this afternoon."

"All right."

"Good. We'll drive up through the valley and stop at the flower farm. Ever walked around a flower farm?"

"No."

"Oh, that's a treat. Flowers are so friendly."

"Really?"

"Oh, yes," said Maude, "they're so empathetic."

Later, walking around the flower farm, she elaborated.

"They grow and bloom, and fade, and die, and change into something else. Look at those sunflowers! Aren't they beautiful? I think I'd like to change into a sunflower most of all."

"Why's that?" asked Harold.

"Because they're simple." She smiled shyly. "And because they're tall."

"What's that?"

"Well, I knew at an early age that I was always going to be short. It was a disappointment but there was nothing I could do about it, except make up my mind that it wasn't going to stop me. It hasn't. Still,

I think it might be fun to be tall." She laughed. "But how about you, Harold? What flower would you like to be?"

Harold rubbed his nose. "I don't know," he said. "I'm just an ordinary person." He gestured out at a field of daisies that ran all the way to the hills. "Maybe one of those."

"Why do you say that?" asked Maude, a little perturbed.

"I guess," he answered softly, "because they are all the same."

"Oh, but they're not! Look here." She guided him over to a clump of daisies.

"See? Some are smaller, some are fatter, some grow to the left, some to the right, some even have petals missing—all kinds of observable differences, and we haven't even touched the biochemical. You see, Harold, they're like the Japanese. At first you think they all look alike, but after you get to know them, you see there is not a repeat in the bunch. It's just like this daisy. Each person is different, never existed before, and never to exist again." She picked it. "An individual."

She smiled, and they both stood up.

"Well," Harold said moodily, "we may be individuals, all right. But," he added, glancing out at the field, "we have to grow up together."

Maude looked at Harold. "That's very true," she murmured. "Still, I believe that much of the world's sorrow comes from people who know they are this"— she held the daisy in her hand—"yet let themselves be treated as *that*."

She blinked back the tears that were forming in her eyes and looked out over the thousands and thousands of daisies waving gently in the afternoon sun.

A RED CONVERTIBLE BOUNCED over the dirt curb and swung a quick right. Two panicked cyclists pulled over as the car sped by them and zigzagged down the road.

"Ha!" said Maude, controlling the wheel. "Power steering!"

"Can't you go any slower?" begged Harold. "There's no rush."

"You're right!" said Maude and immediately eased up on the gas. "I do get carried away. I don't approve of rushing and I thank you for reminding me." She smiled at him. "In China they have a saying: 'No man can see himself unless he borrow the eyes of a friend.' I'm beholden to you, Harold."

Harold smiled back.

"Aw, that's okay," he said, and looked out the window.

Driving into town, Maude slammed on her brakes

at a stop sign. The tires screeched. They screeched again as she took off.

"Boy, Maude." Harold sighed. "The way you handle cars. I'm glad we didn't take mine. I could never treat my car like that."

"Oh, it's only a machine, Harold. It's not as if it were *alive*, like a horse or a camel. We may live in a machine age, but I simply can't treat them as equals. Of course," she added, turning on the radio, "the age does have its advantages."

A rock group played loudly. Maude tapped out the rhythm on the steering wheel. "What kind of music do you like, Harold?"

"Well—"

Suddenly Harold was thrown against the door as Maude made a fast U-turn, drove across the street, up onto the sidewalk, and knocked over a mailbox before finally coming to an abrupt halt.

"Did you see that?" she asked.

"What?" said a disoriented Harold. "What happened?"

"Look."

"Where?"

"Over there on the courthouse lawn."

"What is it?"

"That little tree. It's in trouble. Come on."

She got out of the car, followed by a puzzled Harold, and walked briskly over to a small tree.

"Look at it, Harold. It's suffocating. It's the smog. People can live with it, but it gives trees asthma. See, the leaves are turning brown. The poor thing. Harold, we've got to do something about this life."

"But what?"

"We'll transplant it. To the forest."

"But we can't just dig it up."

"Why not?"

"But this is public property."

"Exactly. Come on."

"Wait. Don't you think we should get some tools, maybe? And a sack or something?"

"Yes, you're right. We'll go see Glaucus. Come on."

She started back to the car but Harold grabbed her arm.

"Look!" he said.

Two policemen had come from the courthouse and stopped at the sight of the car. They were already walking around it and taking notes.

"It's the police," said Maude, nonchalantly. "Come on. They're old friends."

She walked toward them while Harold trailed apprehensively behind.

"Good afternoon, officer. Bit of trouble here?"

"Yes, ma'am," said the policeman, tipping his hat. "Somebody had some trouble parking."

"Well, it's a tricky turn."

"Uh, yes, ma'am," he said, not quite understanding.

"Tell me," said Maude, pointing to the vehicle in front, "is that car parked all right?"

"Oh, yes. That's fine."

"Good. Thank you."

She started off and turned back. "Um, officer. You might turn off the radio. It saves the battery." She smiled at him and walked away.

The policeman turned off the radio. He watched the little old lady take a ring of keys from her coat pocket and open the car door. She hopped inside and opened the other door for the rather nervous-looking youth.

"Nice old gal," said the second officer, coming over from noting the damage to the mailbox. "She reminds me of my grand—"

A screech of tires and a roar of exhaust cut off the rest of his sentence. They looked up to see Maude zoom away from the curb, pop into second, and swing around the corner.

"Forget it," said the second officer after a moment. "My grandmother never learned to shift."

THEY ARRIVED AT GLAUCUS' STUDIO after nightfall. A gas jet on the wall cast the only light, but a large heating unit was going full blast. The block of ice in the center of the room had been chipped down to a mere five feet and was rapidly melting away in the heat. On the corner platform, covered with rugs and skins, Glaucus snored loudly, bundled up in a parka and a New England hunting cap with the flaps pulled over his ears. Asleep, he looked much smaller and more frail. He still held a mallet and an ice pick in his gloved hands.

"Oh, my," said Maude. "We're too late."

"Is he all right?" asked Harold.

"He's fallen asleep, as usual." She took the tools from his hands and began removing his boots. "No matter. We'll come back in the morning."

Harold strolled over to the block of ice. "What is this he's working on?" he asked.

"An ice sculpture. It's Venus—the goddess of love. To get it completed is his unfulfilled dream."

"It is kind of rough," said Harold, trying to make out the figure.

"He's never finished one yet. Look around. He's got every kind of tool known to man, but the poor dear has difficulty staying awake." She finished tucking a rug around him and walked over to Harold.

"Look," said Harold. "The ice is melting."

"I know," said Maude. They watched it for a moment. "That's one of the drawbacks of the medium."

HAROLD SAT BEFORE THE FIRE in Maude's living room and looked at the flames dancing around the log.

"A little after-dinner liqueur?" asked Maude, bringing over a decanter from the sideboard.

"Well, I really don't drink."

"Oh, it's all right. It's organic."

She poured him a drink and handed him the glass. She poured one for herself and then sat down in the easy chair opposite him.

"Let's have a toast, Harold," she said. "To you. As the Irish say, 'May the path be straight because your feet have trod it.'"

"Thank you," said Harold and sipped his drink. "It's nice."

"I'm glad you like it."

He smiled at her.

She smiled back.

He settled into his chair and gestured above the fireplace. "What's that up there?"

"My umbrella?"

"Yes."

"Oh, that's just an old relic. I found it when I was packing to come to America. It used to be my defense on picket lines, and rallies, and political meetings—being dragged off by the police or attacked by the thugs of the opposition." She laughed. "A long time ago."

"What were you fighting for?" asked Harold.

"Oh, Big Issues. Liberty. Rights. Justice. Kings died and kingdoms fell. You know, I don't regret the kingdoms—I see no sense in borders and nations and patriotism—but I do miss the kings. When I was a little girl in Vienna, I was taken to the palace for a garden party. I can still see the sunshine on the fountains, the parasols, and the flashing uniforms of the young officers. I thought then I would marry a soldier." She chuckled. "My, my. How Frederick would chide me about that. He, of course, was so serious, so very tall and proper. Being a doctor at the university, and in the government, he thought dignity was in how you wore your hat. That's how we met. I knocked off his hat. With a snowball in the Volksgarten." She smiled as she remembered. "But that was all . . ."—she gazed into the fire—"before."

As Harold looked at her she suddenly seemed very small and fragile. He felt tongue-tied and uncertain.

"So you don't use the umbrella any more?" he said, breaking the silence.

She looked at him. "No," she said softly. "Not any more."

"No more revolts?"

"Oh, indeed!" said Maude, sparking back to her old self. "Every day. But I don't need a defense any more. I embrace! Still fighting for the Big Issues, but now in my small, individual way." She smiled. "How about a song, Harold?"

"Well, I don't . . ."

"Oh, come on," said Maude, going over to the piano. "Don't tell me you don't sing. Everybody can sing." She sat down and sang a little ditty which began:

"A robin's chirp is the song of the morn,
The nightingale blows an evenin' horn,
A peacock's trill is a thrill stillborn,
But the cuck-cuck-cuckoo
SINGS THE LIVELONG DAY!"

When she had finished, Harold laughed and clapped his hands. "What's the name of that?" he asked.

"It doesn't have one. I wrote it myself."

"I like it."

"Good! Let's play it together."

"But I don't play anything."

Maude sat up. "Not anything! Dear me, who was in charge of your education? Everyone should be able to make some music. It's the universal language of mankind. It's rhythm, harmony, the cosmic dance. Come with me."

She went into the bedroom and opened a large closet, full of all kinds of musical instruments—horns, strings, drums, tambourines. She rooted about for a while and pulled out a banjo.

"Here we are," she said. "Just the thing. Now, you hold it like this and put your fingers like that."

She showed him how to play a couple of chords, and then they went back to the living room.

"Now, remember," said Maude, sitting down at the piano. "Don't just strum it. Be impulsive. Be fanciful. Let the music flow out of you freely, as though you were talking. Okay?"

"All right."

"Okay. From the top. Let's jam!"

With a flourish she began the song, singing the lyrics while Harold strummed carefully along. He managed to keep up with her and they ended together.

"But the cuck-cuck-cuckoo,
'Spite his rote note yoo-hoo,
The cuck-cuck-cuckoo
SINGS THE LIVELONG DAY!"

He looked at her, beaming with delight.

"Okay?" he asked.

Maude whistled. "Superb," she said.

AFTER BREAKFAST HAROLD SAT by the pool and practiced his banjo. He played Maude's song over and over but never to his satisfaction. His unlimber fingers kept missing the chords, and the tune was practically unrecognizable.

"Harold," called his mother from the terrace. "Harold!"

He hid the banjo behind a bush.

"Ah, there you are," said Mrs. Chasen, coming through the rose garden. "I have the most wonderful surprise for you. It's a little present which I know you'll enjoy. Come with me."

Harold followed his mother around to the garages.

"There we are," said Mrs. Chasen, gesturing dramatically. "Isn't it darling?"

She pointed at a brand-new green Jaguar XKE.

"It's for you, dear. I had them tow away that monstrous black thing of yours and leave this in its place. This is so much nicer, don't you think? And so much more appropriate for you."

Harold started to say something.

"Oh, one more thing," interrupted his mother. "I've talked on the phone with your second computer date, and she seems a very nice, quiet young lady—not at all hysterical like the first one. She will be here tomorrow afternoon, and I thought we might have sandwiches and coffee in the library. Now please, Harold. Let's be on our best behavior and make her feel at home. Good-by, dear. I'm off to the hairdresser's." She took a parting look at the XKE. "Cute little thing, isn't it? I like it very much."

Harold stood for a moment, looking at his new car. He made a decision and walked into the garage.

He took off his jacket and wheeled out to the Jaguar a large acetylene torch. Scanning the car, he made a few rough calculations. Then he fired the torch and pulled the great welding mask over his head.

MAUDE ENTERED GLAUCUS' STUDIO. "Good morning," she said.

Glaucus, spryly dressed for autumn, chipped happily away at a new nine-foot-tall block of ice.

"Come in! Come in!" he shouted, not looking around. He made a sweeping scratch across the ice with a metal spoon and stood back to examine it.

"Have you seen Harold?" asked Maude.

"One moment," said Glaucus, and made another scratch on the ice. He stepped back. This time he was satisfied and jumped down from his stand.

"Ah, Madame M! Greetings," he cried, kissing her hand. "As Odysseus said to Penelope—"

"Sorry I'm late," said Harold, rushing through the door.

Glaucus looked up. "A rather free translation, but none the less correct. And greetings to you, too, my gangling young friend."

"Good morning," said Harold. "Hello, Maude."

"Hello, Harold. Ready for today's Operation Transplant?"

"Well, I'm ready, if you are."

"Aha!" said Glaucus, pounding him on the back. "The spirit of Agamemnon and the courage of Achilles! Come here, my boy. Now tell me," he asked, gesturing at the ice. "What do you see?"

Harold looked. "A block of ice," he said.

"Exactly! Now, ask me what I see."

"What do you see?"

"I see the eternal goddess of beauty and love. I see Aphrodite, the consummate woman, full of warmth and fire—*frozen.*" He picked up a small pneumatic drill, shouting, "And it is I who shall set you free!"

Attacking the ice, he made an incision and stepped back to appraise it. He wiped his brow.

"Each morning I am delivered of a new block of ice. Each evening my eyes grow weary, my hands hang heavy, and I am swept down Lethe to slumber—while my goddess, half born, drips away—unseen, unsung, and unknown."

He stopped, overcome with feeling.

"May we borrow a shovel?" asked Maude sweetly.

"Wait!" cried Glaucus. "Let me think. Do I need a shovel today? No! I need a blowtorch." He grabbed a blowtorch, saying, "Take any shovel you want. You are welcome."

"Thank you, Glaucus," said Maude, picking up a shovel. "We'll see you later. Come on, Harold."

"Good-by, Glaucus," said Harold, and they both left.

"Farewell," cried Glaucus, absently. "Farewell, my friends."

He fired the blowtorch and approached the ice.

"'Where'er he moved, the goddess shone before,'" he quoted, adding in a reverent whisper, "—Homer."

MAUDE DROVE THE PICKUP TRUCK at a steady speed along the highway. She looked over at Harold.

Harold smiled. "So far, so good," he said, and glanced out the rear window at the little tree standing upright in the back.

"How's the patient?" asked Maude.

"The tree's fine," said Harold, "but the cop looks kind of mad."

"What cop?"

"The one following us," answered Harold glumly.

The motorcycle policeman drove up alongside Maude and flagged her over to the side of the road. He parked his bike and came up to Maude's window.

"Lady," he said coolly, "you were going seventy miles an hour in a forty-five-mile zone. Could I see your license, please?"

"Certainly," said Maude. "It's on the front bumper."

"No," said the policeman patiently, "I want *your* license."

"You mean those little pieces of paper with your picture on it?"

"Yes."

"Oh, I don't have one."

"Come again?"

"I don't have one. I don't believe in them."

The cop looked at his boots and then off down the road. He adjusted his sunglasses.

"How long have you been driving?" he asked.

"About forty-five minutes, wouldn't you say, Harold? We were hoping to start sooner, but, you see, it's rather difficult to find a truck."

"Could I see your registration?"

"I just don't think we have one, unless it's in the glove compartment. Would you look, Harold?"

"Isn't this your vehicle?"

"No, no. I just took it."

"Took it?"

"Yes. You see, I have to plant my tree."

"Your tree?"

"Well, it's not really mine. I dug it up in front of the courthouse. We're transplanting it. Letting it breathe, you know. But, of course, we would like to get it into soil as soon as possible."

The cop adjusted his gun belt and scratched his nose. He looked down at his boots again.

"Lady," he said slowly, "let me get this straight."

"All right, then," said Maude, starting up the engine. "And we won't take any more of your time." She threw the gear into first. "Nice chatting with you," she cried, and zoomed off.

The cop spun around as the truck sped by. He watched for a moment, speechless. Then he ran to his motorcycle, hopped on, and gave chase.

"I think he's following us," said Harold, uneasily shaking his head.

"Is he?" said Maude cheerfully. "Is that his siren? My, my. How they do like to play games. Well, here goes."

Maude changed gear and accelerated to top speed. Careening down the highway, she dodged cars and changed lanes. The cop on the motorcycle stayed with her, his siren screaming like a soul from hell. Suddenly, Maude made a hard left turn, sending the truck screeching in a half circle. She raced back down the highway, passing the cop on the other side of the road. Cars pulled over out of her way, while the cop made a similar U-turn and darted after her. Maude immediately made another screeching U-turn and flew off in her original direction. The cop, taken unawares, tried to follow her, but the traffic around him was in total confusion. He dodged an oncoming Ford, ran up over the embankment, and finally halted, sliding and spinning, in a muddy ditch.

Harold turned around to face front and cleared his throat. "He's stopped," he reported.

Maude laughed and slowed down. "Ah, yes," she said. "The old double U-turn. Gets them every time."

She drove down the highway and turned off the road to the National Forest.

THEY FINISHED PLANTING the little tree in a pleasant glade, and Maude patted the earth around its trunk.

"There we are," said Maude, standing up. "I think it will be very happy here."

"It's a nice spot," said Harold, leaning on the shovel. "Good soil."

"Yes, it is. I like the feel of soil, don't you? And the smell. It's the earth. 'The earth is my body. My head is in the stars.'" She laughed. "Who said that?"

"I don't know."

"I suppose I did," said Maude, and laughed again. "Well, farewell, little tree. Grow up tall, and change, and fall to replenish the earth. Isn't it wonderful, Harold? All around us. Living things! Come. I want to show you something."

She led him along a trail till they came to a large pine.

"How's that for a tree?" she said.

"It's a tall one."

"Wait till you see the view from the top."

"But you're not going to climb it, are you?"

"Certainly. I do it every time I come here. C'mon, Harold. It's an easy tree to climb."

"But suppose you fall?"

Maude had already started up. "I don't think about it," she answered. "That's unprofitable speculation and not worth my trouble."

She looked down at Harold. "Are you coming yourself, or will you only hear about it secondhand?"

Harold shook his head. "Okay," he said, and started up.

They climbed to about eighty feet. It wasn't difficult, but, as he followed Maude up higher, he felt the tree swaying in the wind. He swallowed.

"Here we are, Harold," said Maude. "It's like a natural perch, just for us."

She sat out on a bough and made room for Harold. He climbed alongside her and sat down, keeping a firm grip on the trunk.

"Isn't it exhilarating?" said Maude, looking out over the forest that stretched for miles to the distant mountains.

"Yes." Harold gulped. "It's high."

"Imagine! Here we are, cradled in a living giant, looking over millions of others—and we're part of it."

"It takes your breath away," said Harold. "It's also windy."

"Yes. We should hoist sail and strike out for the

horizon. Wouldn't that be fun? I used to love sailing. Especially when we couldn't see land, and we were all alone, surrounded by the wide, flat sea. Then we would harness the wind and cut through the waves like galleons bent on discovery."

"When was this?"

"Oh, in the twenties, around the south of France and off Normandy. I remember it was frowned upon. Considered frivolous, or dangerous, or unbecoming— one of those terms that the moribund use to keep the adventurous in tow. But we'll pull them along anyway, won't we, Harold? We'll hitch them to our balloon."

"You could," said Harold. "But I don't know about me."

"What do you mean?"

The wind died down. Harold loosened his grip on the tree. "Well," he said. "Most people aren't like you. They're locked up in themselves. They live in their castles—all alone. They're like me."

"Well, everyone lives in his own castle," said Maude. "But that's no reason not to lower the drawbridge and go out on visits."

Harold smiled. "But you agree that we live alone. And we die alone. Each in his own cell."

Maude looked over the forest. "I suppose so. In a sense. That's why we have to make them as pleasant as possible—full of good books and warm fires and memories. Still, in another sense, you can always jump the wall and sleep out under the stars."

"Maybe," Harold said. "But that takes courage."

"Why?"

"Well, aren't you afraid?"

"Of what? The known I know, and the unknown I'd like to find out. Besides, I've got friends."

"Who?"

"Humanity."

Harold smiled. "That's a lot of friends. How do you know they're all friendly?"

"Well, the way I figure it, we're all the same, and it's just a question of us getting together. I heard a story once in the Orient about two architects who went to see the Buddha. They had run out of money on their projects and hoped the Buddha could do something about it. 'Well, I'll do what I can,' said the Buddha, and he went off to see their work. The first architect was building a bridge, and the Buddha was very impressed. 'That's a very good bridge,' he said, and he began to pray. Suddenly a great white bull appeared, carrying on its back enough gold to finish construction. 'Take it,' said the Buddha, 'and build even more bridges.' And so the first architect went away very happy. The second architect was building a wall, and when the Buddha saw it he was equally impressed. 'That's a very good wall,' he said solemnly, and began to pray. Suddenly the sacred bull appeared, walked over to the second architect, and sat on him."

Harold started laughing so hard that he had to hold onto the tree. "Awww, Maude!" he cried. "You just made that up."

"Well," said Maude, laughing with him. "It's the truth. The world needs no more walls. What we've all got to do is get out and build more bridges!"

THEY DROVE HOME in the late afternoon, taking the same roads as they took before. Maude drove at her usual pace and talked happily to Harold about children's games and how she had taught Frederick to play marbles when they were in hiding after the *Anschluss*. Neither she nor Harold noticed the motorcycle cop giving out a ticket to a car parked by the side of the road.

"What happened to your husband?" asked Harold.

"He was captured," she said, "and shot. Trying to escape. At least that's what they told me later. I guess I never will know the real story."

"Was that in France or Austria?"

Maude did not get the chance to answer. The motorcycle cop, his lights flashing and siren wailing, drew alongside and frantically gestured for her to pull over. She did, and he parked behind her. He got off his bike and with large steps walked to the truck.

"Okay, lady. Out!" he said.

"Hello," said Maude, not quite recognizing him. "Haven't we met before?"

"None of that, lady. Out." He opened the door.

"Oh, well. It must have been your brother."

"Out!"

Maude stepped out. "But there is a family resemblance," she insisted.

"You too, buster," the policeman said to Harold. "Stand over here."

Harold came around the truck and stood by Maude. The cop hitched up his gun belt and took out his citation book.

"Lady," he said. "You're in a heap of trouble. I have you down here for several violations: speeding, resisting arrest, driving without a license, driving a stolen vehicle, possession of a stolen tree—where's the tree?"

"We planted it," said Maude.

The cop glared at her through his sunglasses. He looked in the back of the truck. "Is this your shovel?" he asked.

"No," said Maude.

The cop threw down the shovel. "Possession of a stolen shovel," he noted.

"Officer," said Maude, "I can explain. You see—"

"Lady, you don't seem to realize. Resisting arrest is a serious criminal offense. Under the state penal code, section one forty-eight, paragraph ten—"

"Oh, don't get officious," said Maude, interrupting him. "You're not yourself when you're officious. But then, that's the curse of a government job."

The cop stared at her for a long count. He adjusted his stance. "Lady," he said patiently, "is it true you are driving without a license?"

"Check," said Maude, equally patiently.

"And that truck. Is it registered in your name?"

"Oh! Not in my name."

"Then whose name is it registered in?"

"Well, I don't know. Do you know, Harold?"

Harold didn't know.

"Where are the papers?" asked the cop.

"I suppose they are in the truck. Uh, are you going to take a lot of time with this?"

"Wait here," said the cop, and climbed into the front seat.

"Because if you are—"

"Lady! For Pete's sake. Be quiet."

The cop opened the glove compartment and began looking through the papers. Suddenly he heard the start of an engine. He looked up. Maude was on the motorcycle, revving it up and motioning Harold to jump on behind her.

"Get the shovel!" she cried.

Harold hesitated. The cop was sliding himself out of the front seat. Harold grabbed the shovel, climbed on the bike, and Maude shot off down the road in a cloud of dust.

The cop took out his gun. "Stop! Stop! Or I'll shoot," he cried.

He fired several shots after them.

Maude began defensive zigzag maneuvering. "This is just like the Resistance," she shouted back to Harold.

The cop watched them disappear over the hill. He raced to the truck and climbed inside to start it. He banged his fist on the dashboard. Maude had taken the keys.

IT WAS EARLY EVENING by the time Maude drove up in front of Glaucus' studio and parked. Harold helped her off the bike.

"My, those motorcycles are awfully chilly," she said, laughing. "But aren't they fun!"

"What are you going to do with it?" asked Harold.

"I don't know. I'm going down to the ships tomorrow to say good-by to some friends. Would you like to come?"

"Thanks, but I can't. I have to work on my car. Maybe we could get together the day after."

"Splendid," said Maude. "We'll have a picnic."

They opened the door to the studio and went inside.

Old Glaucus, bundled up in his winter clothes, was valiantly fighting off sleep. He staggered toward the diminishing block of ice, lifted his heavy hammer and chisel, and struck a blow. He turned around and shuffled back to look at its effect. All the time he mumbled snatches of Homer for encouragement.

"'The bitter dregs of Fortune's cup to drain.'— Iliad. . . . Almost finished. . . . Gotta make it. . . . Going to make it. . . . Liberate Love. . . . Set her free."

"Good evening, Glaucus," said Maude.

"We've brought back your shovel," said Harold.

Glaucus looked at them vaguely. "Shovel? 'Shovel the fires till one falls, wrapt in the cold embraces of the tomb!' Excuse me. I must turn up the heat." He faltered over to the thermostat, and turned it up full.

He came back to the ice. "Create." He sighed. "'Verily these issues lie in the lap of the gods.'" He collapsed in a nearby chair. "Just going to sit down for a minute," he muttered. "Won't even shut my eyes."

Harold looked closely at the ice. "I think I see it," he said to Maude.

"Yes," she agreed. "It's almost there."

Glaucus stood up, his eyes barely open. He shuffled in place and made a few swipes at the air with his tools. "Yes," he mumbled. "Not giving up. . . . Almost done. . . . Almost finished."

He wandered over to his large couch and sat down. "Just a little rest. . . . Not long. . . . Then, once more up the hill. . . ." His voice trailed off, and his head fell forward on his chest. He began to snore.

"I think he's asleep," Harold whispered.

"Aha! Morpheus!" shouted Glaucus, popping up, wild-eyed. "I'll beat . . . I'll never . . ." His eyelids closed. "Gonna make it. . . . Gonna make it. . . . Make it. . . ." He plopped on the couch and drifted back against the cushions. It was over. He had fallen asleep.

Harold took the tools from his hands, and Maude made him comfortable on the couch, loosening his boots and covering him with a rug.

As they turned to go, Harold took a last look at the ice sculpture.

"It's melting away," he said.

"Yes," said Maude.

"Don't you think we should turn off the heat?"

"Why?" asked Maude. "There'll be a new block of ice in the morning."

FOR DINNER THAT EVENING Maude decided to go Japanese. She gave Harold a kimono to wear, and she put one on herself. It was a beautiful robe ("a gift from an admirer," she said), made of blue and white silk that matched the colors of her eyes and hair. A friendly dragon was embroidered on the back.

They had supper by lantern light in the Japanese nook, and afterwards she explained to Harold how she had fallen in love with the Orient during the many trips she and Frederick made there after the First World War. Indeed, she confessed, her contact with the East had made a profound impression on her life and, striking a match, she lit up her hookah.

Harold leaned back on the cushions and thought over the day.

"I like Glaucus," he said.

"Yes," said Maude, puffing away pleasantly, "so do I. But I think he is a little . . . old-fashioned." She gestured at the hookah. "Like a drag, Harold?"

"Well, I really don't smoke."

"Oh, this isn't tobacco. It's a mixture of grass and poppy seeds."

"But I've never smoked that kind of . . ."

"It's all right," said Maude, offering him the hose. "It's organic."

Harold took the hose and inhaled. He smiled. "I'm sure picking up on vices," he said.

"Vice? Virtue? It's best not to be too moral. You cheat yourself out of too much life. Aim above morality. As Confucius says, 'Don't simply be good. Make good things happen.'"

"Did Confucius say that?"

"Well. . . ." Maude smiled. "They say he was very wise, so I'm sure he must have."

Harold looked at her intently. "You are the wisest person I know," he said.

"Me!" cried Maude. "Ha! When I look around me, I know I know nothing. I remember, though, once long ago in Persia we met a wise man in the bazaar. He was a professional and used to sell his wisdom to anyone willing to pay. His speciality for tourists was a maxim engraved on the head of a pin—'The wisest,' he said, 'the truest, the most instructive words for all men at all times.' Frederick bought one for me, and back at the hotel I peered through a magnifying glass to read what it said: 'And this too shall pass away.'"

Maude laughed. "And the wise man was right. Apply that, and you're bound to live life fully."

Harold sucked thoughtfully on the pipe. "Yes," he said sadly. "I haven't lived." He took a deep breath. He suddenly giggled. "But I've died a few times," he declared.

"What was that?" asked Maude.

"Died," said Harold happily. "Seventeen times— not counting maimings." He laughed wildly, obviously feeling the effect of the hookah. "Shot myself in the head once with a popgun and a pellet of blood."

"How ingenious!" cried Maude. "Tell me about them."

"Well, it's a question of timing and the right equipment. . . . You really want to hear about this?"

"Of course."

Harold grinned. "Okay," he said, and leaned forward eagerly. "The first time it wasn't even planned. I was at boarding school and they were getting ready for the Centennial Celebration. They put all the fireworks and stuff in the west wing below the chemistry lab. Well, I was in the lab cleaning up, and I decided to do a little experimenting. I got all this stuff together and started measuring it all out. I was very scientific. Then, suddenly, there was this big fizzing sound and this kind of white porridge stuff came slurping out of the beaker and ran along the table, onto the floor. So I took the hose."

Harold stood up to demonstrate.

"I turned it on to wash the stuff into the sink, and POW! There was this massive explosion. It cracked the table, blew a hole in the floor. Knocked me against the wall. Smoke and stink everywhere. I got up. I was stunned. Then suddenly—bombs started going off. Flames shot up through the floor, and PACHAU! skyrockets and pinwheels were flying about the room. Fireballs whizzing and bouncing. Singed my hair. I couldn't get to the door. But behind me was the old laundry chute, so I slid down it to the basement. And when I got outside—wow! The whole top of the building was on fire. It was crazy! Alarms ringing, and people running about. Boy! So I decided to go home."

He sat down by Maude and brushed his hair off his forehead.

"When I got there my mother was giving a party, so I crept up the back stairs to my room. Then there was a ring at the front door. It was the police. I leaned over the banister and heard them tell my mother that I had died in an accident at school. I couldn't see her face, but she looked at the people around her and began to stagger."

Speaking very softly and slowly, Harold continued, tears welling in his eyes.

"She put one hand to her forehead. With the other she reached out, as if groping for support. Two men rushed to her side, and then—with a long, low sigh— she collapsed in their arms."

He stopped for a long pause.

"I decided then," he said solemnly, "I enjoyed being dead."

Maude said nothing for a moment. Then she spoke quietly.

"Yes. I understand. A lot of people enjoy being dead. But they're not dead, really. They're just backing away from life. They're players, but they think life is a practice game and they'll save themselves for later. So they sit on the bench, and the only championship they'll ever see goes on before them. The clock ticks away the quarters. At any moment they can join in."

Maude jumped up, shouting encouragement. "Go on, guys! Reach out! Take a chance! Get hurt, maybe.

But play as well as you can." Leading a cheer before a packed stadium, she cried, "Go team, go! Give me an 'L.' Give me an 'I.' Give me a 'V.' Give me an 'E.' L—I—V—E. LIVE!"

She sat down beside Harold, very ladylike and composed. "Otherwise," she informed him, "you'll have nothing to talk about in the locker room."

Harold smiled. "I like you, Maude," he said.

Maude smiled back. "I like you, Harold. Come, I'll teach you to waltz."

She gave him her hand and together they walked to the Victrola. She turned it on, and the lilting melodies of Strauss filled the room. Taking the hem of her kimono in her hand, she held out her arms. He put his arm around her waist and took her hand in his. He looked down at her and grinned. Her head barely came up to his shoulder. She counted to the music and then, smiling, she began to move. He picked it up, and before long they were dancing together—round and round the lantern-lit room, happily in step, twirling and circling as effortlessly as young lovers waltzing in a Viennese café.

MRS. CHASEN MET HAROLD's second computer date on the front porch.

"You must be Edith Phern," she said to the

bespectacled little girl with the closely cropped red hair.

"Yes, I am," said Edith.

"I'm Mrs. Chasen, Harold's mother. Harold is out by the garage. Let's go meet him, shall we?"

"All right," said Edith, dropping her purse and spilling out all the contents.

Mrs. Chasen waited till she picked them up, and then together they walked around to the back of the house.

"Harold has a new car," explained Mrs. Chasen. "And he's been tuning it up. He's very mechanical."

"Oh," said Edith. "What kind of a car is it?"

"It's a little Jaguar roadster," said Mrs. Chasen, coming around the corner as Harold put the final polish on his new car.

The car had been somewhat changed. Its back end had been squared off like a small station wagon, its back window was frosted glass with a wreath of ferns etched across it, and the whole car had been redone in black, except for some tasteful chrome trimming on the front and sides, and the velvet curtains, which were a kind of funereal purple.

"It's very nice," Edith said sweetly. "Looks like a hearse."

Mrs. Chasen clenched her teeth and smiled.

Harold looked at her blankly.

"Very unique," Edith added. "*Compact.*"

Despite the blow this mini-hearse had dealt her, Mrs. Chasen managed to remain collected. "Edith," she said serenely, "I'd like you to meet my son, Harold. Harold, this is Edith . . . eh?"

"Phern," said Edith. "I'm very pleased to make your acquaintance."

Harold nodded a greeting.

"Harold, dear," said Mrs. Chasen, "I think you should go wash up and meet us in the library. And remember what I said to you. Let's make Edith feel at home."

Mrs. Chasen had decided on a small buffet luncheon in the library. While they waited for Harold, she offered Edith some sandwiches and poured her some coffee. Edith placed her napkin on her knees and balanced the plate on her napkin. She was a little nervous but she overcame it by smiling pleasantly at everything.

Mrs. Chasen handed her a cup of coffee. "And what do you do, my dear?" she asked.

"I'm a file clerk. At Harrison Feed and Grain."

"Oh, how interesting."

"Yes, it's very challenging," said Edith.

They sipped their coffee.

Edith smiled.

"Well, what is it exactly that you do?" asked Mrs. Chasen, trying once more.

"I'm in charge of all the invoices for the South-west. We supply, for example, most of the egg farmers in Petaluma. So you can *imagine!*" She tittered con-spiratorially and took another sip of coffee.

"Mmm, yes," said Mrs. Chasen.

She smiled at Edith.

Edith smiled back.

"Oh, here's Harold now," said Mrs. Chasen as Harold entered the room.

Edith attempted to stand up to greet him.

"Please, Edith," said Mrs. Chasen. "Don't get up."

Edith sat down. Harold sat between them and rested his arm on a small table. Edith smiled at him, and he smiled back.

"Edith was just telling me about her job," said Mrs. Chasen, as she poured Harold a cup of coffee.

"I'm a file clerk."

"Yes. Henderson Feed and Grain."

"No, Harrison," corrected Edith good-naturedly. "Harrison Feed and Grain. At Hamilton and Fourth. I'm in charge of the invoices. . . ."

She smiled.

Mrs. Chasen handed the coffee to Harold, who placed it on the table beside him.

"And I type up the schedule for the trucking fleet."

"She supplies the whole Southwest with chicken feed," said Mrs. Chasen, rather caustically.

"Well, not the *whole* Southwest," said Edith with a modest snicker. "Although we do have a large business. Barley was very big last week. Fifteen hundred bushels. . . ."

Harold took a large meat cleaver from inside his jacket, swung it high, and cut off his left hand at the wrist. The cleaver embedded itself in the table, and, as he picked up the stump, blood dribbled from the plastic hand.

Mrs. Chasen was astonished. She glared at Harold and slowly shook her head.

Edith, fighting for composure, put down her cup and saucer. She stood up. She smiled. "I think I'd better . . ." was all she was able to say before collapsing in a dead faint under the coffee table.

Harold glanced at his mother.

She looked up, speechless, from the fallen Edith. All she could think of were the words of her brother Victor: "I'd put him in the Army, Helen!"

HAROLD DROVE ALONG in his Jaguar-hearse, explaining to Maude how he made the transformation.

"The back of a Datsun station wagon fitted just fine, and, after welding, I laid down the black Naugahyde roof. Then it was only a matter of incidentals—chrome landaus from a Ford Thunderbird, windows, curtains, and, of course, spray painting and rubbing it out."

"It seems to have worked very well," Maude said.

"Yes. I think I like it better than my old one."

"Oh? Why's that?"

"I guess because I've put a lot of myself into it. Fixing it up and making it run. It runs beautifully. I like working with cars."

"I knew a man once who used to like working with cars. A German, wonderful person, but he would spend all his time fixing his car and making it run beautifully. Then came the war, and he lost his car. He had to walk everywhere, and so he found himself spending his time making his body fit and trim. He fixed it up, and it ran beautifully. After the war, he decided not to go back to cars. 'Cars come and go,' he said, 'but your body is your transportation for life.'"

Harold looked over at Maude. "Are you trying to tell me something?" he asked.

Maude smiled. "I just did," she said.

They drove past rolling hills where cows grazed indolently in the sunshine, and finally settled on a picnic spot near a solitary oak in a large pasture.

After a lunch of bread and cheese, wine, carrots, fruit, and nuts, they settled back on the grass.

"Would you like a little licorice, Harold?" Maude

asked. "It has no nutritional value, but then, consistency is not always a human trait."

Harold took a piece and lay down with his hands behind his head. Maude leaned against the tree and opened her bag. She took out her tatting and began busily working the thread.

"Look at the sky," said Harold, chewing thoughtfully. "It's so big."

"And so blue."

"Beyond the blue is the vast blackness of the cosmos."

"Yes. But speckled with uncountable stars. They're shining right now. We just can't see them. I suppose that's just another instance of all that's going on that is beyond human perception."

"Maude," said Harold, after a pause. "Are you religious?"

"What does that mean?"

"Do you believe in God?"

"Oh, yes! Everyone does."

"Do they?"

"Absolutely. Deep down. It's part of being human."

"Well then, who do you think God is?"

"Oh, He has a lot of names. Brahma, the Tao, Jove. And for the metaphysically inclined, there's The First Cause, The One Reality, or The Eternal Root. For me, I like what it says in the Koran—'God is Love.'"

Harold grimaced. "It says that in the Bible," he corrected. "And anyway, it's just a cliché."

"Well, a cliché today is a profundity tomorrow—and vice versa." She held up her tatting. "Isn't that pretty? I only learned how to do that last year."

"Maude, do you pray?"

"Well, we communicate."

"How?"

"Lot of ways. Through living. Through loving. Different levels of consciousness require different levels of communication. Language isn't the only way of talking."

Harold smiled. "Yes," he said. "There's always waltzing."

"Right," said Maude. "One dances for grace—in the theological sense."

"But where is He? Is He inside us or outside us?"

"Both, I imagine. There is a little God inside us to show us where we've been, and a little God outside us to show us where we're going."

"That's pretty mystical."

"You're right, Harold. It's a mystery. Frankly, I'm not sure if He's Our Father or Our Mother. I only know," she said, patting the trunk of the tree, "He's very *creative*."

Harold laughed and stretched out on the grass. "This is really nice here," he said. "Makes me feel like a kid."

Maude laughed.

"Let's have a race to the top of that hill," he said, leaping up.

"All right," said Maude. "Let me put this away first."

"You know what I'd like to do?"

"What?"

"Cartwheels."

"Well, why don't you?"

"Naw, I'd feel stupid."

"Come on, now, Harold. Everyone has the right to be an ass. You just can't let the world judge you too much."

"All right," said Harold, and he did a very spindly cartwheel. He did another and laughed.

"Want to join me in some somersaults?" he asked.

"No, thanks," said Maude. "I'm going to beat you to the top of the hill."

They raced off, running down the slope, past the cows in the next pasture, and on up the hill. They reached the top together and collapsed, laughing and out of breath.

"My, my," said Maude, lying back on the grass. "I feel I could evaporate."

Harold fell alongside her. "You'd turn into one of those clouds," he said. "I think you'd be a nice cloud. You could float around the skies all day."

"No, not me," said Maude. "I'd be a very bad cloud. I'd always want to dissolve into rain."

THEY SPENT THE AFTERNOON at the beach, running along the sand and tempting the waves to wash over their feet. Then they walked out by the rocks and cliffs and examined the smooth stones in the tide pools.

Later, Maude demonstrated the Tai Chi. "Poetic names for poetic movements," she called it.

"To exercise my transportation," said Harold with a grin.

"Partly." Maude smiled. "But it will also uplift your spirit and bring peace to your mind."

And to the sounds of the sea she taught him, among others, "The Wild Horse Ruffles Its Mane," "Repulse the Monkey," "Jade Ladies at the Shuttle," and "Grasping the Sparrow's Tail."

They sat on an old log to watch the sun go down. It put on a spectacular display, throwing varying hues of red, orange, and purple across the banks of clouds.

"Cumulus and alto stratus," said Maude absently. "Reminds me of Shanghai in the thirties."

"Why's that?"

"Oh, we'd fly out of Hung-Jao in a two-seater. Gliding and looping. Like pearl diving. Or galloping across the desert to touch the setting sun. Now, there's an experience, Harold. The desert! We should go. Though I suppose we couldn't do it before Saturday. What are you doing tomorrow?"

"Oh, I have a luncheon date, with this girl."

"Really?"

"It means nothing. My mother set it up."

"It might mean something to her."

"To my mother?"

"And to the girl. Be kind, Harold. You see, I've lived a long time, seen all that I wished, done all that I could, yet it's been my experience that it's kindness that matters, and kindness is what the world sorely lacks."

The wind blew gently in her hair. Harold reached over and took her hand. He looked down at the wrinkles and the splotches of age, and covered it with his. "You're beautiful," he said.

"Oh, Harold," said Maude. "You'll make me blush. I feel like a schoolgirl."

He smiled and kissed her hand. "Thank you," he said, "for a wonderful day."

"Wasn't it marvelous?" she said. "And now we're seeing it end."

She turned and looked out at the setting sun. "There it goes," she said wistfully. "Sinking over the horizon where we're all going to go. The colors are changing and soon they'll be gone, leaving us with darkness—and stars."

Harold held her hand in his. Glancing down he saw for the first time the tattoo etched on the inside of her arm. It was a number—D-726350. Shocked, he looked up at her face.

She hadn't noticed. She pointed out to sea and cried, "Harold, look!"

A lone seagull flew over the waves.

They both watched it for a moment, soaring freely in the reddening sky.

"Dreyfus once wrote," said Maude softly, "that on Devil's Island he would see the most glorious birds. Many years later in Brittany he realized they had only been seagulls."

She looked at Harold and smiled.

"To me," she said, "they will always be glorious birds."

"HAROLD," SAID MRS. CHASEN, "I cannot impress upon you too strongly the importance of this meeting. She is the last girl. The Computer Dating Company was reluctant to send anyone in view of what they heard. And can you blame them? Why, that poor little Edith left here quite shaken. Fortunately, I was able to demand that the company stand by their original agreement. But kindly remember, Harold, this is your third and final chance."

The doorbell rang.

"There she is now, and look at you. Comb your hair and straighten your tie. Please, Harold, try to take this seriously, if not for your sake, at least for mine."

Mrs. Chasen left the room, and Harold went to the mirror to straighten his tie. He brushed his hair off his forehead and decided, as he looked at himself, that this time he would at least try.

Mrs. Chasen came back with a tall long-haired girl in boots, a leather skirt, and a floppy red hat.

"Harold," she said. "I'd like you to meet Sunshine Doré."

Harold approached them. "How do you do?" he said.

"Can't complain," said Sunshine. She had a wide mouth and large teeth.

"Sunshine is an actress," said Mrs. Chasen.

"I like to think so," said Sunshine, idly swinging the strands of beads that hung around her neck. "I work at it."

"Now, why don't I leave you two alone for a moment," said Mrs. Chasen. "Harold, you could talk in the den, and I'll bring in some drinks. Is lemonade all right?"

"Groovy," said Sunshine.

"Good," said Mrs. Chasen, and left for the kitchen. She turned at the door to prompt her son. "Harold, perhaps Starlight would like a cigarette."

"That's *Sunshine*," said Sunshine.

"Yes, of course," said Mrs. Chasen, and left.

"Would you like a cigarette?" asked Harold as he led her into the den.

"No, thank you. They stain my fingers."

He gestured at the couch. She sat down, and he sat beside her.

"Is Sunshine your real name?" asked Harold, after a pause.

"Well, actually, it was the name of my drama teacher—Louis Sunshine. Perhaps you've heard of him?"

Harold shook his head.

"He's mainly a theater personality. Well, he was such an influence on the development of my instrument—that means my body in theater talk—that when I went to Hollywood and felt the need to express the emerging me in a new form, I took on 'Sunshine.' As a tribute. Doré is my real name. Well, Dore, actually."

She looked around the den. "Gee, what a lovely place you have here." She stood up and walked about. "I mean, it's really well decorated. Nice furnishings. They remind me of the auction at MGM."

Harold swallowed.

"Do you play?" she asked, running her hand along the piano.

"No," said Harold. "I'm learning the banjo. Do you?"

"Oh, I studied the guitar. I had a folk-singing class. But I had to give it up. Gave me calluses on my fingers. As an actress, I can't afford to have a tarnished instrument."

"No," said Harold. "I suppose not." This wasn't easy, he decided. He tried again. "Do you do a lot of acting?"

"Oh, sure. I practice every day. That's the Sunshine Method: Keep your instrument finely tuned. Is this your father?" she asked, picking up a photograph of General Ball.

"No. My uncle."

"He's in the Army! I do so like the military, don't you? Those uniforms make men look so virile."

Harold grimaced.

"I did *What Price Glory?* in summer stock," she said, putting down the photograph. "A great production. I played Charmaine—with a French accent."

She went over to the mantelpiece. Harold sat on the couch, patting his thighs.

"Gee, what a lovely collection of knives. Hunting knives, soldier's knives, antiques. We had a display like this when we did Ibsen's *The Seagull*. May I see them?"

Harold took a deep breath. "That's it," he said.

"That's what?" asked Sunshine.

Harold came over to her. "That's a really good collection of knives," he said. "Allow me." He took one down. "Now, this knife is very interesting. It's a hara-kiri blade."

"Ohhhh," cooed Sunshine. "What's hara-kiri?"

"An ancient Japanese ceremony."

"Like a tea ceremony?"

"No. Like this." With an Oriental scream, he plunged the knife in his belly and dropped to his knees. Bleeding profusely, he continued the upper cut, the side cut, and the gouging, then tumbled forward with a terminal shudder.

Sunshine dropped to her knees, wide-eyed. "Oh, Harold," she cried. "That was marvelous! It had the ring of truth. Harold. Please. Who did you study with?"

She drew back. "I'm sorry, Harold," she whispered, self-reproachfully. "I don't want to break into your private moment. I know how exhausting true emotion can be. I played Juliet at the Sunshine Playhouse. Louie thought it was my best performance."

Harold heard her throw off her hat and rearrange her hair. In seconds she had transformed herself into Juliet, and, as her unbelieving Romeo listened, she acted out her final scene in that tragic drama.

"What's here" she cried. "A cup! Closed in my true love's hand? Poison, I see, hath been his timeless end.

Oh, churl!" She whacked him. "Drunk all, and left no friendly drop to help me after? I will kiss thy lips."

Harold opened his eyes, terrified.

"Happily, some poison yet doth hang on them, to make me die with a restorative."

She kissed Harold, who immediately got up.

"Thy lips are warm," whispered Sunshine to the gallery.

Harold backed away, knocking over the telephone table.

"Yea, noise!" shouted Sunshine. "Then I'll be brief." She picked up the knife.

"Oh, happy dagger!" she cried. She took a moment out to test it, pushing the blade into the handle and seeing how it squirted out blood. Satisfied, she continued.

"Oh, happy dagger!" she cried. "This is thy sheath." She pounded her chest. Then, with a mighty thrust and an accompanying gulp, she stabbed herself between the beads and breasts.

She paused to catch her breath. "There," she whispered, clutching the knife to her bosom and staggering to the couch. "There rest . . ." She collapsed across the couch, languidly draping her hair over the end.

"And . . . let . . . me . . . DIE!" With a last toss of the head, she expired, the bloody dagger clenched in her bloody fist and stuck in her bloody chest.

Harold had never seen anything like it. He wandered around the couch, bewildered.

Mrs. Chasen entered with a tray of drinks, took one glance at the couch, and dropped them all.

She looked at her son and flung out an accusing arm. "Harold!" she cried, exasperated. "That was your last *date!*"

GENERAL BALL'S ADJUTANT unlocked the file cabinet marked *Top Secret* and took out the draft file of Harold Chasen. He locked the cabinet and brought the file into the General's office.

The General stood before a mirror with his coat off, adjusting his mechanical arm.

"Here's the file, sir," said the adjutant, putting it down on the desk.

"Oh, good work, Rodgers. Come over here for a second, will you? I think I have a screw loose, or something."

MRS. CHASEN ASKED HAROLD to meet her in the den before dinner. Standing regally in front of him, she delivered her verdict.

"Harold, I spoke with Dr. Harley today, and it seems you have missed your last two appointments.

That information, coupled with your recent behavior, particularly your performance here this afternoon, has left me with no recourse but to listen to the solution proposed by your uncle. Consequently, I have instructed him to take the necessary measures for you to be inducted into the service and, as soon as possible, to take up active duty with the United States Army."

Harold stood up, thunderstruck.

"This was a difficult decision for me to make," she added. "But it is for your own good. I only hope that they have more luck with you than I."

The next day Harold found Maude helping Madame Arouet in her garden. Madame Arouet was putting up bean poles and stringing between them bits of cloth and tin. Maude was over in a corner, clearing the weeds for a new vegetable patch.

"Maude," said Harold, "I must speak to you."

"What is it, Harold?" she asked.

"They're going to draft me. In the Army. I'm going to be sent to war for the government."

"They can't do that," said Maude, completely unperturbed. "You haven't voted."

"But they have," said Harold.

"Oh, well," she said, "don't go. Perhaps today war

is part of the human condition. But it shouldn't be encouraged. Bring over that wheelbarrow, would you please, Harold?"

Harold swallowed. He went and got the wheelbarrow. "If I don't go," he said, "they'll put me in jail."

"Really?" said Maude, forking the weeds into the wheelbarrow. "Well, historically, you'd be in very good company."

She laughed and paused to wipe her brow. "Would you like to do a little hoeing, Harold?" she asked. "Work, I'm told, done with no selfish interest, purifies the mind. Apparently, you sink your separate self and become one with the universal self. On the other hand, senseless labor is an insult and a bore and should be scrupulously avoided."

"Maude. Please!" said Harold. "Do you think you could help me?"

Maude leaned over her pitchfork. "Harold," she said, smiling, "with your skill and my experience—well, I think we can come up with something."

HAROLD SAT NEXT to his uncle in the back seat of the general's limousine. As they drove through the city, he listened attentively as his uncle spoke of the glories of an Army career.

"Harold," said Uncle Victor, "I want you to look

on me as a father in this matter. We'll spend the day just getting to know each other. Now, I know that you have no great desire to join the Army. Hell, I felt the same way myself, when I started out. But my father set me straight, and look at me now—a general! With a chauffeur. Respect. Money in the bank." He patted his empty sleeve as he took out a cigar. "Oh, it has its drawbacks. Like anything else, I suppose. But the Army takes care of you. Believe me. Once you get to know it, you'll love it. By the way, where do you think we should go?"

"I was thinking maybe up to McKinley Park," said Harold. "We could walk around there and talk."

"You mean by the McKinley Dam? Good idea. That's a lovely spot. Hear that, sergeant? McKinley Park."

The general lit his cigar. "Yes, indeed, Harold. You join up, and you've got a buddy for life."

They arrived at McKinley Park, and left the car and chauffeur. As they walked along the path, General Ball looked over at the mothers with their small children, and the senior citizens basking in the sun.

"This is what we're defending, Harold," he said. "Look around you—everything that's good and beautiful in the American way of life. People enjoying their freedom."

"Yes, Uncle."

"Call me 'sir,' Harold. First thing you learn in the Army—an officer deserves your respect."

"Yes, sir."

"Good boy. Ah, look at that old gazebo. I remember in the old days they'd have a military band there on Sundays, playing marches and other patriotic songs. Wait a minute. Is that some peace nut over there? My God, it is! Let's go off this way, Harold. Those crazy Commie bastards. I don't know why we tolerate 'em."

Harold looked over at the peace petitioner.

"Parasites," said Uncle Victor.

"Yes, sir," said Harold, and followed him along the path.

They walked toward the reservoir. The general talked expansively, and Harold seemed to become more and more interested and involved.

"Well, let's examine the facts on it," said Uncle Victor. "I say this country has been too harsh in its outright condemnation of war. I say you can point to many material advantages brought about by a crisis-and-conflict policy. Hell, World War Two gave us the ballpoint pen. That's common knowledge."

"During wartime the national suicide rate goes down," offered Harold.

"Is that a fact? Well, that fits in right along with everything I've been saying. War is not all black."

"Yes, sir," said Harold. "It makes you think."

"Damn right it does. War is part of our heritage. And it's a crying shame the way it has been handled in the last few decades. I mean, let's look at it out in the open. Let's stop this pussyfootin' around. Can you tell me why the hell we've given up on the Germans? Can you? Those damn politicians in Washington have chalked them up on our side, and the wars ever since have been a national disgrace. Hell, look at history. The two best wars this country has fought were against the Jerries. Now *I* say, get the Krauts back on the other side of the fence where they belong, and let's return to the kind of enemy worth killing and the kind of war this whole country can support."

"Wow, sir," said Harold. "That's pretty strong stuff."

"Well, Harold," said Uncle Victor, breathing deeply and absently patting his empty sleeve, "I've always been a man who speaks his mind. It's hurt me. I'm not liked in Washington. I know that. But—and you ought to remember this—I do have friends in high places."

They walked along the reservoir and sat on a small hill beneath a tree. No one was about, and the general began telling Harold some of his wartime experiences.

"They came at me from all sides. Hundreds of 'em. We kept firing. Zat-tat-tat-tat! 'Throw the grenades,'

I shouted. 'Mac, throw the grenades!' 'He's dead,' Joe said, and kept right on feeding me the bullets. Zat-tat-tat-tat! They kept falling, but they kept coming. Bullets whizzing all around me. Zot! Joe falls back with a neat red hole in his head. I thought I was done for. But I kept firing. Zat-tat-tat-tat! Only one thought kept me going. Kill! Kill! For Joe and Mac and the rest of the guys. Kill!—a blinding flash. I wake up on a stretcher. 'Did we hold?' I asked the medic. 'Yes, sir,' he said, and I slipped into unconsciousness."

"Gee! That's a great story, sir."

"Well, you'll soon have stories like that to tell of your own."

"You think so, sir?"

"Sure. You'll be able to tell your children. Something for them to look up to. Be proud of."

"I hope so, sir. Golly, I never knew it could be so exciting."

"It's the greatest excitement in the world."

Harold sat up and mulled it over. "To pit your own life against another," he said pensively.

"That's right."

"To kill."

"Yes, indeed."

"The taste of blood in your mouth."

"The moment of truth."

Harold took hold of an imaginary rifle and aimed

it at an imaginary enemy. "Another man's life in your sights."

"Yes."

He pulled the trigger. "Zap!"

Uncle Victor laughed.

"Will they really teach me to shoot?" Harold demanded.

"Oh, sure," said Uncle Victor. "A variety of weapons."

"And to use the bayonet? AHHHHHH!"

"Oh, sure."

"How about hand-to-hand combat?"

"You'll have plenty of that."

Harold grappled with an imaginary victim and began to kill him. "To strangle someone. Choke him. Slowly. Squeeze out his life between your hands."

Uncle Victor looked at Harold and became slightly perturbed.

"Eh?" he said.

"How about to slit his throat?"

"Well, I don't . . ."

"I'd like that. You could see the blood squirt out."

"Harold. I think you're getting carried away here."

"Sir, how about souvenirs?"

"Souvenirs?"

Harold sprang to his knees. "Of your kill. You know—ears, nose, scalp. Privates."

"Harold!"

"What's the chances of getting one of these?" he asked, and pulled out a shrunken head. "Wow! To think maybe I could make my own."

"Harold!" cried Uncle Victor. "That's *disgusting!*"

"It certainly is!" said Maude.

Harold and the general stopped talking and looked up. Maude stood over them, her goose-head umbrella in one hand and a large peace sign in the other.

"Who are you?" asked Uncle Victor, standing up.

"I am petitioning for peace, and I came over here—"

"Parasite!" shouted Harold, jumping up and thrusting his fist in Maude's face. "Parasite!"

"Harold, control yourself," said Uncle Victor.

"Commie bastard!" cried Harold. "Get out of here!"

"Don't you talk to me like that, you little foul-mouth degenerate," said Maude. "Really, General, I thought you at least—"

"Traitor!" shouted Harold. "Benedict Arnold! Remember Nathan Hale, right, sir?"

"Don't you advance on me!" Maude shouted.

"We'll nail every last one of you! You're all going to end up like *this!*" And he held up the shrunken head.

"Filth! Filth!" cried Maude.

"Lady, please," said Uncle Victor. "Harold—"

"Just like this," said Harold, shaking the shrunken head in Maude's face.

"Give me that!" she cried, and grabbed it out of his hand. "I'm going to throw this in the sewer where it belongs." She turned and ran off toward the reservoir.

"She took my head," said Harold, dumbfounded.

"Stay where you are," ordered the general.

"She took my head!" screamed Harold. He picked up Maude's fallen peace sign and ran after her. "I'll kill her!" he screamed.

"Harold, come back! Harold, that's an order." The general followed him in hot pursuit.

Maude ran past the sign saying "Danger—No Trespassing!" and under the fence that led to the dam. Harold followed her, wielding the peace sign like a club. The general, totally unnerved, ran after them.

Scampering out along the edge of the dam, Maude stopped in the middle and held the shrunken head out over the rushing water below.

"Don't you dare!" cried Harold, catching up with her and grabbing her arm. Maude clobbered him with her umbrella, and when the general arrived she clobbered him too.

"Lady, please," cried Uncle Victor, trying to restrain Harold with his one arm. "Give him back the head."

"I'll kill her," shouted Harold. "I'll kill her!"

"Keep away from me, you twisted little pervert!" screamed Maude.

The general wrenched the peace sign from Harold and threw it over the dam. They paused for a moment to see it disappear in the treacherous water below. Maude stood on the general's right, holding the shrunken head. With a quick move, Harold pulled the general's lanyard which activated his mechanical salute. The sleeve sprung out and clipped Maude under the chin, knocking her over the dam and into the churning waters. The general, horrified, watched her go under. He waited anxiously, but she did not come up.

Still with his sleeve held at salute, he looked up. He couldn't believe what he'd seen. He turned to Harold for some reason for this calamity—some motive, some explanation.

"I lost my head," said Harold sadly, and watched the water flow rapidly downstream.

BACK AT HEADQUARTERS General Ball sat at his desk. "You can get rid of the Chasen file," he said to his adjutant. "My nephew is not going in the Army."

"Shall I put it back in Top Secret, sir?"

"No need to, Rodgers. Send it back through regular channels and have it certified medically unfit for active duty."

"Anything specific, sir?"

"Use your own judgment, lieutenant. But, confidentially—the boy is an idiot. A homicidal maniac. He belongs in a mental institution."

"Yes, sir. Here's the latest body count, sir."

"I shudder to think, Rodgers, what would happen to the Army if we allow it to become a refuge for killers."

Two SKELETONS, hung on two doors, jingled their bones and laughed uproariously. The doors burst open and Harold and Maude went scuttling by in a small cart that drew up by a sign marked "Exit." An attendant helped them out of the cart, and they walked down the steps to the promenade.

"Well, so much for the Haunted House," said Harold. "It wasn't very scary."

"No," said Maude. "It had nothing on this afternoon."

"Oh, you weren't scared."

"Scared? Swimming underwater with that oxygen device of yours? I was petrified."

"Go on, you loved it."

"Well, of course, it was a new experience."

They both laughed. Harold bought tickets for the

Ferris wheel, and they were helped to their seat and locked in.

"Off we go!" said Maude, as they sailed above the carnival lights and up into the night sky. "Isn't this fun? I used to ride the Prater wheel all the time."

"Too bad you lost your umbrella in the reservoir," said Harold.

"Oh, well," said Maude. "It served its purpose. That's all you can ask of anything—or anybody."

"Your plan certainly served its purpose. If you could have seen my uncle's face." Harold laughed. "The Army won't want me now."

Maude laughed too. "Well, the Army was all right in its day," she said. "Like the Church. Together they protected us from the bad guys on the one hand and the devil on the other. But—as everything will—the foe has changed. We have met the enemy and he is us. So we'll just have to sit down now and reason out some better solutions than defenses with weapons and dogmas."

"Do you think we'll succeed?"

"Oh, certainly. Keep the faith! The way I see it we're now in the cocoon. The day of the caterpillar is over. The time of the butterfly is at hand."

"Oh, we've stopped," said Harold.

"And right at the top. What fun!"

"Look at the people down on the pier. They seem so small. Maude! Wait! What are you doing?"

"Just rocking the boat," cried Maude, wildly swinging the seat.

Harold was very relieved when they stepped off the Ferris wheel and went into the penny arcade.

They played the pinball machines and tested their grips. But it was the hand-operated soccer game that gave them the most fun.

Maude right away got into the football spirit. She cheered her team on enthusiastically and manipulated her men to kick goal after goal.

Fifteen minutes later a crowd had gathered around her. A short Italian man played with her against a couple wearing matching Hawaiian shirts. The crowd cheered on every play and slapped each other on the back whenever a goal was scored.

Harold stole away and put a penny in a machine that stamped out letters on a metal disk. As he marked the letters and pulled the lever, he listened to the cheering and smiled.

"You sure have a way with people," he said as they left the amusement park and walked along the pier.

"Well," said Maude, "they're my species."

Harold bought two candy apples, and they sat out on the end of the pier to eat them.

"Look!" said Harold, pointing. "A shooting star!"

"I saw it," said Maude. "My, my. There's always an oddball, even in the firmament."

Harold looked up at the stars. "They're beautiful, aren't they?"

"Yes. They're old friends. I used to watch them in Bavaria. They can be very . . . comforting."

"How do you mean?"

"Well, for example, I used to look up and think that light traveling from a distant star would take over a million years to reach us. In a million years Nature evolved the wing of a bird. So, maybe by the time that light reaches us, mankind will have learned to deal with evil. Maybe he will have phased it out altogether, and we'll all be flying around . . . like angels."

Harold smiled. "You should have been a poet."

"Oh, no!" cried Maude. "But I should have liked to be an astronaut. A private astronaut, able to just go out and explore the unknown. Like the men who sailed with Magellan. I want to see if we really can fall off the edge of the world."

She laughed. "What a joke it will be," she said, making a large circle with her candy apple, "if, like them, I end up where I began."

"Maude," said Harold.

"Yes."

"I have a present for you." And he handed her the metal disk.

"Oh, Harold! How nice." She read the inscription out loud. "'Harold loves Maude.'"

Harold, somewhat embarrassed, turned and looked out to sea. Maude touched his arm, and he turned around.

"And Maude loves Harold," she said softly.

He smiled, and Maude gave a happy laugh.

"Oh, my!" she said. "This is the nicest present I've received in years." She kissed it and tossed it into the ocean. Harold watched it go in disbelief.

"But . . ." he said.

"Now," explained Maude, "I'll always know where it is."

Harold swallowed. "Okay," he said, and smiled.

"Come on," said Maude. "Let's try the roller coaster."

And hand in hand they walked back along the pier to the dazzle of the carnival on the boardwalk.

BACK AT HER PLACE, Harold lit a fire while Maude prepared her chrysanthemum cordial in the kitchen (a pound of chrysanthemums, water, sugar, lemon peel, nutmeg, and a pint of quality brandy).

"It's delicious," said Harold.

"Oh, I love cooking with flowers," said Maude. "It's so Shakespearean."

She turned on the radio in the bookcase. "I think

there's a Chopin concert on FM tonight. Yes. There
we are."

The delicate sounds of a nocturne flowed out into
the room.

"Do you like Chopin, Harold?"

"Very much."

Maude sat on the piano stool and sipped her cordial. "So do I," she said. "So do I."

Harold walked over to her and leaned on the
piano. He looked at the empty frames.

"Why are there no photographs in these frames?"
he asked.

"I took them out."

"Why did you do that?"

"They mocked me. They were representations
of people I dearly loved, yet they knew these people
were gradually fading from me and that, in time, all
I would have left would be vague feelings—but sharp
photographs. So I tossed them out. My memory fades,
I know. But I prefer pictures made by me, with feeling,
and not by Kodak with silver nitrate."

Harold smiled. "I'll never forget you, Maude," he
said. "But I would like a photograph of you."

Maude laughed. "Well, let me see."

She put down her glass and went into the bedroom. By the closet with the musical instruments
stood an old sea chest.

"Bring over the candelabra," said Maude, kneeling

down, "and we'll get some light on this. How's the banjo coming?"

"Just fine," said Harold, taking the branched candlestick from the bedside and bringing it over to Maude. "I'm going to surprise you tomorrow night."

"My, my." She chuckled, opening the chest. "It's going to be quite a birthday celebration. I'm certainly looking forward to it."

She shuffled through old papers, bundles of letters, and well-worn manila envelopes. "It's in here somewhere," she said.

"These candles smell nice," said Harold, standing over her. "What is that incense? Sandalwood?"

"Yak musk," said Maude. "But I don't think they call it that commercially. It's 'Fragrance of the Himalayas,' or something. 'The Dalai Lama's Delight.' I suppose that's nicer."

"It's more romantic."

"Pay dirt!" cried Maude, holding up a large envelope and closing the trunk. "I think it's in here."

She got up and sat on the canopied bed. Harold put down the candelabra and sat beside her. She opened the envelope. "Yes. Here it is," she said. "My American visa."

She peeled the photograph off the document and handed it to Harold. "On short notice, this is the best I can do."

"Thank you." He held it up. "Very pretty. It looks just like you."

Maude smiled. "Harold, that picture is almost twenty-five years old."

"You haven't changed a bit. I'll keep it in my wallet."

He opened his wallet and out fell a picture of a sunflower, clipped from a dealer's catalogue. He quickly retrieved it and turned away from Maude.

"You're not supposed to see that," he said, putting it back in his wallet. "It's another part of tomorrow night's surprise."

He closed his wallet and turned back to Maude.

"Maude," he said. "You're crying."

Maude held the visa in her hand. "I was remembering how much this meant to me," she said slowly. "It was after the war—I had nothing—except my life. How different I was then. And yet how much the same."

Harold was perplexed. "But . . . you've never cried before. I never thought you would. I thought you could always be happy."

"Oh, Harold." She sighed, stroking his hair. "You are so young. What have they taught you?" She brushed away the tears that fell down her cheeks. "Yes. I cry. I cry for you. I cry for this. I cry at beauty—a sunset or a seagull. I cry when a man tortures his brother . . . when he repents and begs forgiveness . . . when forgiveness is refused . . . and when it is granted. One laughs. One cries. Two uniquely human traits. And the main thing in life, my dear Harold, is not to be afraid to be human."

Harold blinked away the tears in his eyes. He had a lump in his throat. He swallowed. Reaching out, he took her hand in his. Then, gently touching her cheeks, he brushed away her tears.

She smiled slightly, and he leaned forward and kissed her on the lips.

Parting, they looked at each other in the candlelight. They heard the Chopin playing softly in the next room. Leaning forward, Harold took her face in his hands and kissed her again. Her arms embraced him tenderly. As effortlessly as two raindrops merge, they fell back together on the canopied bed.

HAROLD AWOKE the next morning to the crowing of a rooster—"Cock-a-doodle-doo!"

He rubbed his eyes and yawned. He heard it again. Taking care not to wake Maude, he sat up in bed and looked out the window.

Madame Arouet was feeding her chickens, and her rooster, perched on a fence post, was greeting the new day.

As Harold watched, the line of a song ran through his head:

"A rooster crows to bravissimos,
But the cuck-cuck-cuckoo . . ."

He smiled and scratched his chest. He felt great. He stretched. He thought he'd like a cigarette. He looked back down at Maude.

The morning sun shone on her white hair and threw a soft golden glow about her face. She slept like a child, he thought, serene and secure. He had never seen anything more beautiful.

He snuggled down beside her and pulled up the covers. He laid his head in front of hers and waited for her to wake up.

She opened her eyes. They were as clear and sparkling as a mountain stream.

She smiled.

"Good morning," she said.

"Happy birthday," he said, and kissed her on the nose.

MRS. CHASEN SAT in her bedroom, eating her breakfast and talking on the phone.

"And so I thought, Father, that you, being a man

of the cloth, might be able to speak to him. Frankly I'm at my wits' end."

Harold, knocking on the door, came into the room.

"Mother."

Mrs. Chasen waved him off. "No, Father. He will not be going into the Army just at present. Apparently his uncle thinks it is unwise at this time."

"Mother."

Mrs. Chasen covered the mouthpiece. "Not now, Harold, I'm talking to Father Finnegan."

Harold folded his arms.

"Mother," he said, "I'm going to get married."

"Father, I'll call you back," said Mrs. Chasen, and hung up.

"What did you say?" she asked.

"I'm getting married."

Mrs. Chasen looked at him carefully. "To whom?" she inquired.

"To a girl," said Harold, taking out his wallet. He flipped it open and handed it to his mother.

Mrs. Chasen took one look at the photograph and closed her eyes. "I suppose you think this is very funny," she said.

"What?"

Mrs. Chasen handed him back the wallet. "A picture of a sunflower."

"Oh, sorry," said Harold, and flipped over to the photograph of Maude. "Here she is," he said, and handed it back to his mother.

This time Mrs. Chasen examined it closely. She looked up at him and then examined it again.

"You can't be serious?" she said faintly.

Harold smiled.

"He's serious," she said to Dr. Harley, as she lay on his couch, looking up at the ceiling. "He's *actually* serious."

"I'll have a talk with him," said the doctor. "Maybe I can do something."

"Oh, I hope so. I sincerely hope so. I'm sending him to you, his uncle, and to Father Finnegan. Surely someone can talk sense into him."

Uncle Victor certainly gave it a try.

"Harold," he said to his nephew, seated in his office before him, "your mother has told me about your marriage idea, and though, normally, I have nothing against marriage, I don't think this one is quite normal. Helen says your fiancée is eighty years old. Now, even to an untrained mind, this is not the customary relationship. In fact, dammit, it's highly irregular.

Now, I don't want to remind you of the unpleasant incident that happened yesterday. I think it is best if we consider that forgotten. Nevertheless, knowing your peculiar bent, I think that it would be wisest for you not to leave the house or indulge in any kind of activity that would be newsworthy. This marriage would attract attention, and in my opinion, Harold, you don't need a wife. You need a *nurse.*"

The meeting with Dr. Harley was much cooler.

"There's no doubt, Harold," said the doctor, leaning back in his chair, "that this impending marriage adds another chapter to an already fascinating case. But let us examine it, and I think you'll realize there is a simple Freudian explanation for your romantic attachment to this older woman. It is known as the Oedipus complex, a very common syndrome, particularly in this society, whereby the male child subconsciously wishes to sleep with his mother. Of course, what puzzles me, Harold, is that you want to sleep with your *grandmother.*"

The session with Father Finnegan never seemed to get off the ground. The little priest seemed overcome by the enormity of the problem.

"Now, Harold," he said, patiently. "The Church has nothing against the union of the old and the young. Each age has its own beauty. But a marital union is concerned with the conjugal rights. And

the procreation of children. I would be remiss in my duties if I did not tell you that the idea of . . ."
He swallowed.
". . . *intercourse*—the fact of your young, firm . . ."
Lowering his eyes,
". . . body . . ."
He stroked his forehead.
". . . *co-mingling* with the withered flesh, sagging breasts, and flabby buttocks of the mature female person— . . ."
He rubbed his hand despairingly across his mouth.
". . . frankly and candidly, makes me want to *vomit.*"

"BUT," SAID HAROLD to all three of them when they had concluded their statements, "you didn't ask me if I loved her."
And neither General Ball, nor Dr. Harley, nor Father Finnegan could find an answer for that.

"LOVE!" CRIED MRS. CHASEN, throwing up her arms. "What do you mean 'love'? Really, Harold, how can you talk of love when you know nothing at all about it?"
"I know what I feel."

"You think that's love? That's not love. That's some geriatric obsession! How can you do this to me? I don't understand it. I simply don't understand it."

Mrs. Chasen went to the bar and poured herself a drink. In all the years he had known her, Harold had never seen her so distraught. It struck him as ironic, because all that didn't matter any more.

"Harold," she said, sitting down beside him. "Listen to me. Why do you want to throw your life away?"

"I'm just going to ask her to marry me."

"But what do you know about her? Where does she come from? Where did you meet her?"

"At a funeral."

"Oh, that's wonderful." Mrs. Chasen took a drink. "I not only get an eighty-year-old daughter-in-law. I get a pallbearer as well! Harold. Please. Be reasonable. Think what you're doing. What will people say?"

"I don't care what people say."

Mrs. Chasen stood up. "You don't care! 'Senior Citizen Weds Teenage Arsonist in Funeral Chapel!'— And you don't care!" She walked to the bar.

Harold had had enough. He got up to go.

"All I want is for you to marry a nice girl, have a nice wedding—what are you doing?"

"I'm leaving," said Harold.

"You're walking out?"

"Yes," he said.

"But, where are you going?"

He turned in the doorway. "I'm going to marry the woman I love."

Mrs. Chasen stopped. "Harold," she said very quietly. "This is insane."

Harold smiled. "Perhaps it is," he said, and closed the door.

THAT EVENING HAROLD opened the door of Maude's cottage and led her in blindfolded.

"Hold on to my hand," he said, guiding her to the center of the room.

"Oh, I love surprises," she confessed gleefully. "They make me feel so—chiffon!"

"Okay," said Harold. "Stay there." He took off her mask. "Da-dum!"

Maude blinked and looked around. "Oh, Harold!" she said, joyfully clapping her hands. "They're beautiful!"

A hundred sunflowers filled the room—on the tables, the chairs, the mantelpiece—and over the fireplace was a banner saying "Happy Birthday Maude."

Maude walked around the room, dazzled and delighted. She laughed. "They're so gorgeous. Where did you get them all? You must have planned this for days."

"I have," said Harold, and turned on the Victrola. A Strauss waltz floated out across the room.

"May I have this dance, sweet lady?" said Harold, making a courtly bow before her.

Maude curtsied. "With all my heart, kind sir," she replied.

He took her in his arms, and they waltzed merrily till the record ended.

"And now," said Harold, drawing back the Japanese screens. "Supper for two."

"My, my!" cried Maude, totally enraptured. "Silver place settings! Where ever did you get them? And look at that."

Harold picked up the small silver vase with a single daisy in it and presented it to her. "From me to you," he said. "An individual. Remember?"

Maude took the daisy and held it gently in her hand. "Thank you," she said. "I do."

"And now," said Harold, dramatically flinging off the cover over the ice bucket.

"Champagne!" cried Maude, delightedly. "Oh, you've thought of everything."

Harold picked up the bottle and began to remove the cork. "It's all right," he said, imitating her accent. "It's organic."

Maude laughed. "Oh, wait," she said, and rushed into the bedroom. "I have a surprise for you, too." She came back with a box. "Aren't birthdays fun?" she said. "To me they always meant a new beginning, another year of adventure!"

"Watch out," cried Harold. The cork flew from the bottle and the champagne fizzed over the brim. He poured it quickly in her glass and filled up his own.

"You can open this after dinner," said Maude, putting her present on the mantelpiece.

"After the concert," said Harold, handing her a glass of champagne.

"All right," she said. "You make the toast."

Harold held up his glass. "To us," he said.

"To us."

They sipped their champagne and smiled.

"Finally," said Harold, "I have one more surprise." He took from his pocket a tiny ring box, wrapped with a little red ribbon. "You can open it after my solo," he said, putting it beside Maude's gift on the mantelpiece.

"I hope," he added, looking at her tenderly, "it will make you very happy."

"Oh, I am happy," said Maude. "Ecstatically happy. I couldn't imagine a lovelier farewell."

"Farewell?"

"Why, yes. It's my eightieth birthday."

"But you're not going anywhere, are you?"

"Oh, yes, dear. I took the pills an hour ago. I should be gone by midnight."

"But . . ." Harold stared at her.

Maude smiled and sipped her champagne.

He realized suddenly what she had done.

He bolted to the phone.

THE AMBULANCE RACED through the city streets, its red lights flashing and its siren wailing like a banshee in the night.

Inside, Maude lay on the stretcher, covered with a blanket and happily holding the daisy in her hand. Her only concern was Harold, who knelt beside her, crying piteously.

"Come on, Harold," she said, "give us a smile. What a lot of fuss this is. So unnecessary."

"Maude. Please. Don't die. I couldn't bear it. Please, don't die."

"But, Harold, we begin to die as soon as we are born. What is so strange about death? It's no surprise. It's part of life. It's change."

"But why now?"

"I made up my mind long ago that I'd pick the date. I thought eighty was a good round number." She giggled, suddenly. "I feel giddy," she said.

"But, Maude, you don't understand. I love you. Do you hear me? I've never said that to anyone in my life before. You're the first. Maude. Please. Don't leave me."

"Oh, Harold, don't upset yourself so."

"It's true. I can't live without you."

Maude patted his hand. "'And this too shall pass away.'"

"Never! Never! I'll never forget you. I wanted to marry you. I was going to ask you tonight. Don't you understand? I love you. I love you."

"Oh, that's wonderful, Harold. Go—and love some more."

The ambulance drove up to the Emergency entrance of the hospital, and the attendants ran around and opened the back.

"So unnecessary," giggled Maude, as they slid her onto a gurney and wheeled her inside.

Harold walked beside her. "Hold on," he said. "Just hold on!"

"Hold on? Hold on?" Maude giggled again. "Oh, Harold. How absurd!"

The attendants wheeled her to the receiving desk and left to fill out their forms. An officious redheaded nurse stood behind the counter, explaining to a student nurse the hospital's admitting procedures.

Harold anxiously banged on the counter and a young intern with horn-rimmed glasses looked up from his book.

"Please," said Harold. "There's been an accident,

an overdose of pills. We've got to see a doctor. It's an emergency."

"Very good," said the head nurse. "Now, Julie, you go ahead and get all the particulars."

The student nurse took out her clipboard and picked up a pencil. "Ah, what's your name?" she asked pleasantly in a slow Southern drawl.

"It's not me," said Harold. "It's her."

Maude stopped her humming and smiled. She waved "hello" with her daisy.

"It's better to begin," said the head nurse, "by asking the last name first, then first name, then middle initial, if any. It saves time."

"Oh, right," said the student nurse. She smiled at Maude. "What is your last name?"

"Chardin. The Countess Mathilda. But you may call me Maude."

"Oh, thank you."

"Please!" cried Harold. "She has got to see a doctor right away."

"Young man," said the head nurse, "perhaps you ought to wait in the waiting room."

The student nurse had written down Maude's name. "How old are you?" she asked.

"Eighty. It's my birthday."

"Oh! Many happy returns."

"No. I don't think so."

"You don't understand," cried Harold. "She's taken an overdose of pills two hours ago. She hasn't got much time."

The intern came from behind the counter with his clipboard and asked Maude for her signature. "It's just a formality," he explained.

"Be delighted to," said Maude, signing it with a flourish. "I like your hair so much," she added.

"Really," said the intern. "I'm letting it grow long. Now, this form is just in case of a damage claim. You know, so the hospital won't be responsible for . . . whatever."

"I think, Julie," said the head nurse, "it's better to use a ballpoint pen. They're more efficient."

"Oh, right."

"Purely a legal safeguard," continued the intern, checking over the signature. "Nothing personal, you understand."

"Don't you all realize?" cried Harold. "She's dying."

"Well, not *dying*, actually," Maude explained. "I'm changing. You know, like from winter to spring. Of course, it is a big step to take."

"Perhaps, then, Julie, you'd better skip the preliminaries and get to the important section."

"Oh, right," said the student nurse, and conscientiously turned over the page. "What is your Social Security number?"

"No," said the head nurse. "Ask about the insurance. The hospital insurance."

"Oh, right. Do you have any insurance? Blue Cross? Blue Shield?"

"Insurance against what?"

"No insurance," said the student nurse. She turned sadly to her superior.

"Well, write it down."

"*This is madness!*" shouted Harold.

"I'm sorry," said the head nurse, giving Harold an icy stare, "but the psychiatrist won't be in till morning."

"What's the trouble here?" asked a doctor, coming through the swinging doors.

"An overdose of drugs, doctor," said the head nurse.

Harold went up to the doctor while the student nurse leaned over and asked Maude solicitously, "Do you have a welfare plan at your place of employment?"

"I'm retired," said Maude.

"Doctor, please," said Harold. "She's swallowed these pills. You've got to do something."

"All right, take her in there."

The intern began wheeling her away. "It was nothing personal," he said.

"Who's the next of kin?" cried the student nurse, her ballpoint pen ready.

132

"Humanity," Maude shouted back cheerily as she went through the swinging doors.

"Farewell, Harold," she cried, waving the daisy. "I'm off for the new experience." The doors swung shut behind her.

Harold stood and watched till the doors had stopped swinging completely.

IT WAS ELEVEN O'CLOCK on the waiting room clock. Harold noticed the sweep second hand was broken.

He sat in the corner. A black woman sat across from him, staring stoically at the darkness out the window. Her little boy slept beside her on the couch.

At eleven thirty her elder son came out through the swinging doors, his head and arm in bandages. She said nothing to him. She woke up the little boy and took him by the hand. All three left without saying a word.

Harold sat in the room alone. He glanced at the torn magazines on the table. He rubbed his face. He leaned forward in his chair and stared at the swinging doors.

At midnight the new nursing shift came on.

At one o'clock the intern closed his book and left.

Around three an expectant father and his pregnant wife arrived at the emergency room by mistake. They were given directions for the maternity ward. The father kept apologizing. The wife just smiled. They left. Harold stood up and walked up and down the hall.

At four the janitor came by and emptied the ashtrays.

By five Harold had returned to the waiting room. He sat on the couch and stared at the torn magazines on the table.

By six the night sky had lightened. Harold could make out the shapes of the cars in the parking lot.

At seven twelve the doctor came in to tell him that Maude had died.

He received the news very calmly. His face showed no sign of emotion. He thanked the doctor mechanically and walked away down the hospital corridor.

MAUDE'S LIVING ROOM looked different with the morning sun streaming through the window. The remains of the party were everywhere—the sunflowers, some of them already beginning to droop; the champagne bottle standing half empty in a bucket full of water.

Harold walked to the window. Outside the birds sang and pecked at the birdseed. Idly he flipped the handle of the feeding trolley, remembering the first day he had seen it work. His eyes began to fill with tears. He blinked them away and walked to the fireplace.

Catching sight of the "Happy Birthday" sign, he violently ripped it off the wall. The sunflower pots and everything on the mantelpiece crashed to the floor—including the little ring box, with the red ribbon around it.

Immediately ashamed of himself, he picked it up and saw beside it Maude's present to him from the night before. He put it on the table and opened it up. It contained her ring of car keys, the collection she had received from Sweeney. He looked at it, displaying no emotion, and at the floridly handwritten note attached. "Dearest Harold," it read. "Pass it on—With love, From Maude."

He took the note in his hand and sat down. He read it again. The tears welled in his eyes. This time he could no longer fight them back. He did not even try. She was gone. It was over.

The note dropped from his hand. Falling listlessly back on the couch, he began to cry. She was gone. It was over. He was alone.

The tears ran down his cheeks. His sobbing grew louder and unrestrained. Crying hopelessly, like a lost child, he buried his face in the cushions.

THE MINI-HEARSE sped along the sea-cliff road, recklessly spinning around corners and sliding dangerously close to the edge.

Harold sat at the wheel, driving like a man possessed. The tears were still wet on his face. His hands firmly gripped the wheel. He turned off on a dirt road that led to a high bluff and raced along it till he reached the top.

From far down the coast one could see the car go over. It flew off the cliff, did a gliding half turn, then crashed on the rocks and burst into flames.

The fire subsided, and the smoke and steam gradually disappeared. The waves, brought in on the rising tide, washed in and around the wreckage.

Harold looked down at it from the edge of the cliff. The sun sparkled in the broken glass. A piece of burned curtain drifted back and forth on the swell; overhead, the gulls glided carelessly on the wind.

Harold rubbed his nose and put Sweeney's keys in his pocket. He stretched, took a deep breath, and wiped his tearstained face with both hands. Swinging his banjo from around his back, he strummed a few chords. He took a final look at the remains of his car and turned away.

As he walked down the hill, he began to pluck out Maude's song. He played it through once, remembering in snatches how she had sung the words:

"But the cuck-cuck-cuckoo,
'Spite his rote note yoo-hoo,
The cuck-cuck-cuckoo . . ."

He smiled. He began it again. It was getting better and better, he thought, and he knew he'd have it right before he came to the end of the road.

The Colin Higgins Foundation is the recipient of all royalties for this novel. Screenwriter/director/producer Colin Higgins established the foundation in 1985 after being diagnosed with HIV. He dedicated his foundation to the eradication of AIDS, to helping those with HIV, and to the betterment of the lives and options for the LGBT community. Since his death in 1988, the foundation has given out more than three million dollars to over 340 individuals and groups, including start-up funds for GLSEN (the Gay, Lesbian & Straight Education Network) and the Trevor Project, the first national suicide prevention hotline for at-risk LGBT youth. Other grants include over a decade of scholarships at Stanford, UCLA, and the American Film Institute, as well as helping fund the documentary *Celebrating Laughter: The Life and Films of Colin Higgins*. In addition, the foundation hands out the annual Colin Higgins Youth Courage Awards to outstanding LGBT teenagers who, in spite of intolerance and bigotry, have helped transform their communities for the betterment of all. For more information visit www.colinhiggins.org.